Orlando Furioso is a seminal work of very high order and, most important, it is not one of those classics more admired than actually read. When it first appeared in 1516, it reached, almost immediately, a vast audience and became astonishingly popular throughout Europe. The book had nearly a dozen translations within its first fifty years. Spenser imitated it; Goethe admired it; Cervantes praised it and quoted from it in his own masterpiece of chivalric romance, *Don Quixote*; even Voltaire admitted himself fascinated by Ariosto. Scott learned Italian in order to read it in the original, while Byron, too, learned much from Ariosto.

Orlando Furioso attained such popularity because it is lively and exciting and fun to read. Now this new prose translation can delight and thrill readers of the twentieth century as readers of earlier eras were once delighted.

ORLANDO FURIOSO
Volume I:
The Ring of Angelica

Translated by Richard Hodgens

With an Introduction by Lin Carter

**Adult
Fantasy**

PAN/BALLANTINE

This edition first published in Great Britain 1973 by
Pan Books Ltd, 33 Tothill Street, London SW1

ISBN 0 330 23814 0

Cover design by David Johnston

Made and printed in Great Britain by
Richard Clay (The Chaucer Press), Ltd,
Bungay, Suffolk

Contents

The Ring of Angelica

It has been said of *Orlando Furioso* that it is the greatest sequel ever written. To offset this rather backhanded compliment, let us look at the facts.

Ludovico Ariosto, who was born at Reggio nell' Emilia, Italy, first showed considerable talent as a poet, but seemed unable to fulfill that early promise. In his day—he was born in 1474—the thing to do was to write poems in Latin, like the Roman poets. He tried that first, but his Latin verses were decidedly unmemorable. As one contemporary critic has observed, "In the age of Flaminio, Vida, Fracastoro and Sannazaro, better things were to be expected from a poet of Ariosto's obvious gifts." His lyrical compositions demonstrated his mastery of artifice, but seem unworthy of him. His comedies—he wrote four, all of them best forgotten—are but labored imitations of craftsmen like Plautus and Terence. He seems to have been one of those writers who needed a specific model to follow. He found one in Boiardo.

This Boiardo (Count Matteo Maria Boiardo, born forty years before Ariosto) was the first great verse romancer of medieval Italy. He wrote, or at least began, an extravagant heroic romance for the amusement of Duke Ercole d'Este and his court; the romance was entitled *Orlando Innamorato,* and it was left unfinished

when Boiardo died in 1494. Since these were the care-
free, innocent centuries before the invention of copyright
laws, a lot of versifiers thought it would be a good idea
to take up *Orlando Innamorato* where Boiardo left off
and finish it themselves. None of these efforts were
successful, but it appears that Boiardo's unfinished
work was just the kind of situation Ariosto's talent
had been seeking.

Ariosto was only twenty when Boiardo died, somewhat young to be writing great poetry. Ariosto, in fact,
waited a good nine years before setting himself to the
task, which he began in 1503. What he actually did
was not so much to complete the unfinished fragment
as to use it as the starting point for a virtually self-
contained sequel. In so doing he became one of the
few writers in literature who, in trying to imitate another writer, managed to improve on the writer he was
imitating. (Even Vergil, remember, makes a poor second to Homer.)

Orlando Innamorato was a typical product of its
particular time and place. Boiardo had come along in
the footsteps of another Italian poet named Pulci; Pulci
had written a mock-heroic poem called *Morgante Mag-
giori,* which was essentially a lampoon of the heroic
romances the French poets had been writing a little
earlier about Roland and Oliver and the Twelve Peers
of the Emperor Charlemagne. Boiardo picked up Pulci's
idea, but did his *Orlando* straight (well, fairly straight);
a typical, nobly born Renaissance man of letters, he
wrote poems in formal Latin, admired Herodotus and
Xenophon, whom he translated, and, when it came to
refashioning the basic substance of the French *chansons
de geste,* he introduced the theme of romantic love into
the warlike Carolingian mythos. *Orlando Innamorato*
("Roland in Love") tells how the ravishingly beautiful
Princess Angelica of Cathay arrives at the court of

Charlemagne, accompanied by four grim giants, to get some help for her brother, wrongfully driven from his kingdom. Charlemagne's knights outdo themselves in their offers of help, especially Orlando, or Roland. But the dwarf enchanter, Malagigi, Charlemagne's pet wizard, smells a rat, checks his magic books, and discovers that this lovely Princess is herself a powerful sorceress full of deceit, with a heart as cold as ice, for all that her smile would charm a stone statue. She has come out of Cathay with her brother Argalia, sent into Europe by her father, Galafrone, the wicked and cunning old King of Cathay, to foment trouble among the Christians.

The King of Cathay has armed his daughter with a magic ring of incredible power. Wearing it protects her from every enchantment, and putting it in her mouth makes her invisible. The real idea is that Angelica should lure each of Charlemagne's knights into fighting a joust with her brother Argalia, who, with his magic armor and weapons, and his enchanted black horse Rabicano, cannot lose. Once each and every one of the renowned paladins has become the helpless prisoner of Argalia, Angelica can then dictate terms to Charlemagne. So Malagigi tries to work his own magic on the Princess of Cathay before she can ensnare the entire flower of Carolingian chivalry; unfortunately for the dwarf, Angelica is wearing the magic ring at the time, and takes *him* prisoner instead. She has him transported to Albracca in Cathay, where King Galafrone imprisons him in a cavern beneath the sea.

Charlemagne's knights are eager to joust with Argalia. Astolfo is the first to be conquered; a chivalrous Christian, he yields himself as Argalia's prisoner. But the next to be overcome is the pagan knight, Ferrau; he doesn't give a damn for the laws of chivalry, and instead of yielding himself when unhorsed by Argalia's magic lance, he whips out his sword, takes Argalia by surprise, and beats him. Angelica loses her nerve and, popping the magic ring into her mouth, escapes from the scene invisibly; Argalia seizes the opportunity to scuttle away as well. Ferrau, distinctly annoyed, takes off after them, leaving poor Astolfo the only prisoner. Without, however, a captor, Astolfo eventually picks himself up and goes home. Since his own lance was shivered in the duel with the Cathayan, he takes back with him the magic lance which Argalia has abandoned in his flight.

A couple of Charlemagne's peers, Orlando and Rinaldo, decide to ride after the beautiful blonde Princess and find out what all this is about. Rinaldo, however, runs afoul of a magic fountain left over from a previous mythos (the Arthurian one). Merlin, the legendary magician of King Arthur's court, had made it for Tristram to cure him of his doom-fraught love for Queen Ysolt of Cornwall. Whoever drinks of the icy waters of the magic fountain instantly hates the one he has previously loved. Rinaldo drinks—decides he doesn't care for Angelica at all—and starts back to court. But en route he encounters a second fountain whose waters make you fall madly in love.

Meanwhile, the vengeful Ferrau has caught up with the cowardly Argalia, and fought with him. Seeing her brother getting the worst of it, Angelica runs away again, convinced that Argalia has been killed. Thirsty, she comes to the second fountain, drinks, and, seeing Rinaldo sleeping amid the flowers, falls passionately in love with him. She wakes him up, but Rinaldo, having just drunk of the first fountain, and not having bothered to sample the wares of the second one, sees Angelica, whom he promptly loathes, and leaps on his horse to get away from her. Heartbroken, she heads home, and, the whole plot having fallen through, turns Malagigi loose, on his promise that he will work his magic to send Rinaldo to her, which he does. In Cathay, Angelica wines and dines Rinaldo and tempts him with every wile, but nothing can overcome his detestation of her.

Orlando and Astolfo follow Angelica's trail to Cathay, while another lord, Agricane of Tartary, also captivated by Angelica, makes war on King Galafrone for the hand of his daughter. Charlemagne's peers offer their aid in the war, and fight against Tartary, but with Galafrone's schemes all gone awry, Cathay is left to suffer from the curse of Angelica's beauty. France has not had an easy time of it, either, for with most of his best knights now gamboling around the steppes of Central Asia, Charlemagne has found himself attacked by Agramante, King of Africa, and Marsilio, King of Spain, who have seized this advantageous time to make war on France. Even with Orlando and the other champion knights away chasing after Angelica, the treacherous monarchs of Spain and Africa would not have dared go up against the unconquerable Charlemagne, had they not had sure predictions of success so long as they have a young knight named Ruggiero on their side. He is an invincible warrior, descended from Hector of Troy, and raised by the great magician, Atlante.

Hearing that Charlemagne is hard pressed, the wandering heroes start back to help him. Astolfo has got lost along the way somewhere, but Orlando has managed to get hold of Angelica. The once proud Princess of Cathay has been greatly humbled by now. She has failed to win the heart of her beloved Rinaldo, she believes she has seen her brother slain by the pagan knight Ferrau, her father's kingdom has been knocked apart in the war with Agricane, and agents of Agramante, the African king, have somehow stolen her

magic ring. She promises to go back to France with
Orlando, hoping that Rinaldo will be there.

Once they all get back, however, those two troublesome fountains get into the plot again: Rinaldo drinks
from the fountain of love, and falls headlong for
Angelica; Angelica drinks of the fountain of disdain,
and develops a burning hatred for Rinaldo. Rinaldo
makes a pass at Angelica, who repulses him; Orlando,
who is still obsessed with Angelica (even without the
aid of the magic fountain), is, not unnaturally, more
than a little irked at this and warns his cousin off. They
fight, but as both of them have powerful enchanted
swords, it looks like a draw. Orlando's Durindana and
Rinaldo's Fusberta do a lot of damage to the local
scenery, though, and in the confusion, Angelica makes
her getaway—which is where Boiardo left the story,
and where Ariosto takes over.

Boiardo was no mean writer. His narrative sweeps
along at a steady pace; his poem evokes much scenic
splendor in tournament and banquet; his Orlando is
the perfect model of the courtly hero, marred by the
single flaw of his falling for a heartless and cunning
villainess. In fact, although Boiardo's story has no real
depth to it, it is highly civilized, even sophisticated.
He shows a firm control over motivation (which had
been the weak point with the authors of the original
chansons de geste) and a fine sense of contrast in his
depiction of character—as, for instance, the balance
between the impulsive, impetuous Rinaldo and the
thoughtful, serious, even self-conscious Orlando.

Ariosto continued Boiardo's plot in much the same
idiom, but had a different concept of the characters
which makes it impossible for his poem to be considered
a mere continuation. It is in truth more of an inde-
pendently inspired sequel than a form of posthumous

collaboration. Ariosto was in every respect Boiardo's superior. His narrative has freshness and exuberance, a rare vitality and inventiveness which impelled him to exceed his model in the creation of a far larger cast of characters, a far richer and more varied landscape, and a plot infinitely more complex. Most authorities concede Ariosto to have been the greater artist, surpassing Boiardo in mastery both of language and of scenic effects.

Orlando Furioso ("The Madness of Orlando") was enormously popular, and Ariosto himself became extremely important in the history of Italian literature—in world literature, for that matter; he and Boccacio were the only Italian writers since Dante to penetrate beyond the confines of their native land to achieve a truly international reputation. Ariosto's vast historical significance derives from the fact that with his heroic romance he broke with tradition, and, instead of composing it in Latin, wrote it in Italian. During and after his day, narrative verse continued to be written in Latin, but, as E. M. W. Tillyard puts it in *The English Epic and Its Background* (Oxford, 1954), "The main channel of the creative poetic impulse had been diverted to the vernacular," where it would forever remain.

The first forty cantos of the great *Orlando Furioso* were published in 1516. Later Ariosto added six cantos. He continued working on the poem until the day he died, revising, expanding, polishing, and in the process he created a masterpiece. Even in its original version, however, it almost immediately reached a vast audience and became astonishingly popular throughout Europe. The book appeared in nearly a dozen translations within its first fifty years, and its popularity did not diminish thereafter until the declining decades of the nineteenth century. Spenser imitated it; Goethe admired it; Cer-

vantes praised it and quoted from it in his own masterpiece of chivalric romance, *Don Quixote;* even Voltaire
admitted himself fascinated by Ariosto. Scott learned
Italian in order to read it in the original, while Byron
learned much from Ariosto.

I think that what makes the book live, even today, is
Ariosto's liveliness and sense of humor. *Orlando Furioso*
is not one of those classics more admired than actually
read; it never has been. It is not cold and formal and
classical; in fact, it has been criticized by those who
dwell in the groves of Academe on the grounds that
"it lacks classic solemnity, epic grandeur and epic
simplicity; it lacks the necessary element of tragedy;
it has too much comedy in it."

In other words, it is lively and exciting and fun to
read. True, it is not the world's greatest book. Where
it does fall down is, in my estimate, in the matter of
plot. It doesn't have a balanced plot structure and it
undeniably lacks organic unity. Instead of having a
basic over-all plot to bind the whole work together,
Ariosto just goes on and on, adding fresh inventions,
following the magic lance with the magic ring, the
magic ring with the magic helm, the magic helm with
the magic fountain, reminding one of a cliff-hanger
serial. When he exhausts one character, he sticks in
a new one—until the book teems with giants and fairies
and magicians and phantoms and Saracens. The impact
of *Orlando* is gained through a cumulative richness of
unending invention and elaboration and interweaving
of themes.

But the book demonstrates its author's truly astound-
ing energy and sense of fun. He constructs a vast stage
set, and invents an immense cast to enact an inordinate
variety of roles thereon. In so doing, Ariosto becomes
a major figure in the great tradition of imaginary world

fantasy, a direct ancestor of *The Well at the World's End, The Worm Ouroboros,* and *The Lord of the Rings.*

This translation is an entirely new one, written especially for the Adult Fantasy Series by a young science fiction and fantasy writer, Richard Hodgens, who, while studying Italian, fell in love with the inexhaustible charm of Ariosto.

Hodgens originally wrote to me back in 1969, the first year of the Series; he liked my anthology, *Dragons, Elves, and Heroes,* in which I had selected examples of "Tolkienian" fantasy from such ancient works as the Finnish *Kalevala,* the Welsh *Mabinogion,* the Icelandic *Volsunga Saga,* and the Russian *Kiev Cycle,* to say nothing of Sir John de Mandeville, Ossian and the great Persian fantasy epic, the *Shah Namah.*

Hodgens suggested Ariosto's *Orlando Furioso* as an apt source for material should I be planning another comparable anthology of ancient fantasy from epic, saga, myth and romance. I replied that I was indeed planning a second such compilation, to be called *Golden Cities, Far,* and that I would like to include something from Ariosto, except that all the English translations known to me were dismal attempts to render the sparkling and agile *ottava rima* into lumbering English rhymed couplets. Hodgens came back with an offer to translate some of it into clear English prose, and rendered a sample—Chapter Twelve of the present book—which I heartily enjoyed and promptly inserted in *Golden Cities, Far.* Delighted with the job Richard Hodgens had done on that sample chapter, we signed him to a contract, and he is now translating the entire poem for us.

Our new edition of *Orlando Furioso* will appear in several volumes, of which this is the first.

I hope you enjoy reading it—I certainly am!

—LIN CARTER
Editorial Consultant

Hollis, Long Island, New York

ONE

The Fountain of Disdain

I celebrate the ladies, knights, arms, affairs, ancient chivalries and brave deeds of that time when the Moors of Africa crossed the sea and ravaged France, following the wrath and youthful fury of Agramante, their king, who boasted that he would avenge the death of his father, Troiano, on Charlemagne the Roman Emperor. I shall tell also those truths about Orlando never before put into prose or verse; how love drove him to fury and madness, exceeding wise though he was before he loved. . . . At least, I shall tell you all I promise if the woman who drives me almost as mad with love—troubling my mind, hour after hour—will allow me enough strength and time to finish.

Ippolito, generous son of Ercole, ornament and glory of our age, accept this work penned humbly in your service. I can repay what I owe you only in part with this writing. It is not much; but what little I can give, I do give to you. And among the worthiest heroes I intend to write about you will find Ruggiero, your own ancestor, the founder of the House of Este. You will hear about his great bravery and brilliance, if you listen, if you can put aside your own cares and concerns for a while, or can find time among them for my tales.

Orlando, who for so long had loved the beautiful Angelica, Princess of Cathay, and who had won innumerable immortal trophies for her—in India, in

Media and in Tartary—had now returned with her all
the way back to the West, where he found Charlemagne
encamped with the forces of France and Germany on
a field below the great peaks of the Pyrenees. The
Emperor and his host were waiting there, ready to
make Agramante and his ally, Marsilio of Spain, bitterly
regret their folly in having led their great armies across
the sea and over the mountains to destroy the beautiful
realm of France. Orlando arrived (at long last) precisely at the time when battle was about to be joined—
and soon regretted it.

For then and there his lady was taken away from
him. How often human judgment errs! He had defended her from far eastern to far western shores,
and now, in the midst of his friends, in his own land,
she was taken away, without even the drawing of a
single sword. Wisely, his uncle, the Emperor Charlemagne, wanted to evade a contest over Angelica between Orlando and Rinaldo on that day of battle. Once
before Angelica had come to France, escorted on that
occasion by her brother Argalia. He had lost his life,
but she had distracted all the Emperor's knights with
her beauty. He was not happy to see her again, welcoming only Orlando, gone for so long on account of
her—and now threatening a fight with Rinaldo on
account of her.

Charlemagne did not care for such quarrels, especially not at such a time. He took the lady and put
her in the keeping of the old Duke of Bavaria. Cannily
he then promised her as a prize to the knight who
killed the largest number of infidel invaders in the
great battle (thus proving once again his enormous
capacity for statesmanship).

But it proved impossible for him that day to count
the dead or award any prize. His forces were scattered.
Along with many others, the Duke of Bavaria was

taken prisoner and his pavilion was abandoned in the rout.

There the lady had awaited the outcome, until it seemed clear to her that Fortune was turning against the Christians. Whereupon she mounted a palfrey, watched a while longer, and fled when she had to— into the deep forest by the field. On the narrow path she met a knight coming the other way on foot—all his armor on, helmet on his head, sword at his side and shield on his arm, but running through the wood more lightly than a half-naked athlete racing in an open field for a prize. Angelica wheeled her palfrey round in the narrow way as quickly as though she had stepped on a snake—for the knight was Orlando's cousin Rinaldo, Lord of Montalbano, son of Duke Aimone of Clermont.

Rinaldo, having lost his horse Baiardo in the battle not long before, was looking for the beast. But as Angelica turned to flee, he recognized her—the lady who had once loved him, and whom he now loved so much. He forgot his horse. He forgot his battle. Running even faster, he hurried after his lady.

She turned the palfrey and drove into the depths of the wood, not down the path back to the battlefield. And in the wood she drove not down the safest way, but recklessly, anywhere. Pale, trembling, crazed with fear of Rinaldo, she let the palfrey choose the way in the wilderness, only urging him on with her heels. And he raced on until he came to the bank of a river.

There the pagan Spanish knight Ferrau stood, covered with sweat and dust. He had left the battle a while before and had come to the river to drink and rest. He was still there because in his eagerness to drink he had carelessly let his helmet fall into the stream, and he had not been able to retrieve it. As Angelica burst out of the forest, calling for help, Ferrau jumped up, saw her, and knew her well, though it was many days since he had heard of her, and many more since he had seen her. He was the knight who, hoping to take her when she first came to France, had killed her brother. Further, he had taken her dead brother's helmet and had kept it—until he lost it that day in the river.

And because he was courteous and brave and still wanted her anyway, he answered her call for help as readily as if he still wore her dead brother's helmet, or any helmet at all; drawing his sword, he challenged Rinaldo, who followed close behind her. Rinaldo was not afraid of him. These knights not only knew each other by sight, but had crossed swords before. And just as they were—both on foot and one without a helmet—they began to fight with their naked swords, hammering fiercely at each other's plate and mail. Metal soon buckled and broke; anvils could not have withstood the impact of their swords. And while they fought, Angelica drove her palfrey on through woods and clearings as fast as she could.

After the knights had fought a while in vain, neither wounding nor moving one another, only damaging armor, their skill outwitting their strength, Rinaldo, his voice choked with anger and desire, said to the pagan, "You're harming yourself as well as me by keeping me from her. If this goes on—even if you win—what will it matter? She won't be yours, either; she will be gone. It would be better, if you want her too, to catch her before we settle this and before she goes any farther! When we have her, then we may decide who gets her. Otherwise, I don't know how either one of us will get anything out of this."

The proposal did not displease the pagan. The combat was postponed. In their truce, the knights forgot their anger and hatred so completely that when Ferrau left the riverside on his horse, he did not leave the good Rinaldo behind on foot, but invited him to mount up behind him on the croup—and only then did the two amicably gallop off on Angelica's trail.

The knights of old were very good that way. These two were rivals, they were of different faiths, it was wartime and they still ached all over from the impact of each other's swords on their armor, yet they rode together down a crooked path in the deep woods in perfect trust. Driven by their four spurs, however, the horse soon came to a place where the path divided in two. They did not know which branch to take, since both bore fresh tracks. So they left it to chance. Rinaldo dismounted and walked one way, and Ferrau took the other.

Ferrau was soon bewildered. Circling about, he found himself at the river again—at the same spot where he had dropped his helmet in the water. Having no longer any hope of getting the girl, he went down the bank to the edge where he had knelt to drink and so lost the helmet. He had realized at the time that it was caught in the sandy bottom and knew it would not be easy to recover. Now he took a great branch from a tree and made a long pole to probe the bottom. He searched, but he could neither see it nor feel it with the pole. Still, he was too irritated and stubborn to give up. He persisted until he saw the head and shoulders of a fierce-looking knight emerge from the deeper water in the middle of the stream.

This knight was fully armed, except for his dripping head. But in his raised right hand he held high a helmet—the very helmet that Ferrau had wasted that long afternoon trying to dredge up.

Opening his mouth, waiting only for the water to spew from it, the knight sputtered angrily, "Ah, breaker of your faith and your word! Swine! Why worry about leaving the helmet, too? This helmet, which you ought to have returned to me a long time ago! Remember how you killed Argalia, Angelica's brother? Remember the man you killed? I am he! I am Argalia!

"And remember how you promised to throw my helmet in the river—after my corpse and all my other arms. Now that Fortune has forced you to keep your word at last, do not be so disturbed about it. If you worry yourself about the helmet, worry rather that you broke your word.

"If you want a fine helmet to wear, find another. And wear it with more honor—one like Orlando's, or Rinaldo's. Orlando's helmet was Almonte's; Rinaldo's was Mambrino's. And those Christian knights killed pagan enemies and won the helmets fairly. Get one of them—as fairly. This one, which you gave your word to leave to me, you had better leave to me, after all."

At the sudden apparition of Argalia in the river, the Saracen's hair stood on end, his face lost color and his voice died in his throat. Then, hearing Argalia rebuke him for breaking faith, he burned with shame and anger. Not having time to think of an excuse, and knowing very well that what the apparition said was true, he did not even try to speak before it disappeared —slowly sinking back into the river.

But in his overwhelming shame, Ferrau now swore by the life of his mother Lanfusa never to wear another helmet—except the one that once in Aspramonte, in Calabria, the young Orlando took from the head of the fierce African, Almonte, the brother of that King Troiano whom Orlando also killed when the Africans last invaded Europe. This new vow Ferrau kept better than he had kept the other one to Argalia. He moved away, ever onward, ridden without cease by shame and sorrow, intent only on finding Orlando in order to take the helmet.

A different adventure befell the good Rinaldo, who had walked down the other path; he had not walked far before he saw his destrier Baiardo leaping ahead like a horse wild in the woods again, as when he had first found him, years before.

"Stay, Baiardo! Stop!" he yelled. "I need you!"

But the horse did not listen and did not come to him; instead, it went on even faster.

Rinaldo hurried after, burning now with anger as well as with love.

But we follow Angelica, who had also fled. She fled through dark and frightful forest, uninhabited and wild. The moving leaves and branches of oak, elm and beech all filled her with sudden and constant fear. She fled this way and that, up hill and down, taking strange detours because in each shadow on the hills or in the glens she was fearful of finding Rinaldo—terrified that, for all she knew, he might be right behind her. She fled like a fawn that has just seen a leopard catch its mother by the throat and tear her open, and so flies in panic from grove to grove, feeling the brush of each broken branch as the pitiless teeth of the beast of prey.

All that day and night and half the next day she went on, wandering, not knowing where.

She found herself at last in a grove like a garden, lightly stirred by a benign breeze—like a garden, or even a brilliantly decorated chamber. Two clear streams murmured through, pausing to keep it all fresh and green and making sweet, low music over the pebbles in their beds. Here Angelica felt safe at last, as if she were a thousand miles away from Rinaldo. She was exhausted by fear, flight and the summer's heat, and she told herself she had better rest a while. Dismounting among the flowers, she let the palfrey loose; he went wandering down to the edge of the bright water, where the grass was best. Not far away, Angelica herself came upon a delicious thicket of blooming thorn bushes and red roses beside the mirroring pool. Tall, full oaks shaded it on either side from the hot sun. A hollow in the heart of the thicket made a cool, well-hidden room, with leaves and branches so thick and interlaced that neither the sunlight nor inquisitive eyes could penetrate it. And inside, the short, soft grass made an inviting bed.

The harassed beauty lay down and immediately fell asleep. But not for long; she was soon awakened by the trampling of approaching hoofs. Then there was silence again. Getting up quietly, she peeped out, and saw that a knight in armor had come to the edge of the water.

She did not know whether he was friend or enemy. Fear and hope tore her heart and left her too weak to move. She waited and did not break the stillness of the place with so much as a sigh.

The knight sat down at the very edge of the water and rested his chin on his hands. He remained so lost in thought for so long that he seemed to have been turned into insensible stone. For more than an hour he stayed there, silent and sad. Then he began to lament so softly that the sound would have melted granite with pity, have tamed the wildest tiger. He sighed and wept so profusely that his cheeks resembled rivers, his chest an Etna.

"The thought," he said, "the very thought freezes and burns my heart and gnaws at it so painfully. What can I do, when I have come too late, and someone else has had all the rich spoils—everything! And if

I cannot touch the fruit or flower, why do I, why must I, go on torturing my heart for her?

"A virgin is like a rose, alone and safe in the midst of its own thorns in a fair garden. The soft, gentle breeze and the dewy morning air, the water and the earth yield everything to its favor. Neither shepherd nor flock comes near. Longing youths and maids in love want to wear it.

"But no sooner is it picked from its green stem than it loses all the favor it had of men and of Heaven, and grace and beauty—all lost. The virgin who gives away the rose, which she should value more than her sight—or her life—loses the value she had in all her other lovers' hearts. She is worth nothing to them, to anyone except the one she generously allowed take the rose. . . . Oh, cruel Fortune! ungrateful Fortune! Others triumph and I die of desire! But can I stop wanting her? Can I lose my life itself? Ah, sooner—today!—were my days ended, than I live any longer, if I am obliged not to love her!"

In case anyone is beginning to wonder who this man was, shedding all those tears in the brook, he was the King of Circassia, Sacripante, tormented by love. I should add that love was the sole reason for all his anguish, and that the object of his devotion was Angelica. She knew his voice very well.

For love of her, Sacripante had journeyed from where the sun rises to where it sets. He had learned, in India, how she had sailed for the West with Orlando, and he had followed. Then in France he learned that the Emperor had sequestered her, in order to give her to the nephew—Orlando or Rinaldo—who gave the gold lilies of France most help that day against the Moors. He had been in the field and knew of the cruel rout Charlemagne suffered. He had looked for some trace of the fair Angelica but had been unable to find any. This, then, was the new sorrow that made him lament with words so pitiful that they might have slowed the sinking sun that afternoon.

While he suffered and cried and said a lot of other things that I do not care to repeat, his good fortune brought everything to Angelica's ears. And she paid close attention to his moaning complaint, his look of misery—all because his love for her never slept and gave him no rest. This was not the first time she had heard such things, and not the first time she had heard them from him. But being colder than a marble column, she did not condescend to pity him, or any other man, save for that one time she had loved Rinaldo, before he loved her. She behaved with contempt for everyone; no one in all the world was deemed worthy of her love.

Now, however, lost as she was in the woods, the reunion did not displease her, and she decided she would accept Sacripante as a guide. (A drowning man is proud indeed if he will not ask for help.) She reasoned that if she let this chance go by, she would never again find an escort so reliable. She already knew by long trial—when she was besieged for her beauty in her capital, Albracca—that this king was more constant than any of her other suitors. Not that she intended to ease the pain that consumed him, or compensate his old wounds by giving him the pleasure every lover longs for. Instead, she planned some pretense, some fraud, to keep him dangling just long enough to serve her purpose, when she would once again assume her usual coldness.

Out of the dark, hidden thicket of thorns she stepped —with a display of beauty stunning as if Diana or Venus had suddenly shown herself in the dark wood. And "Peace be with you," she said to him, "and may God preserve my good reputation and not allow—

against all reason, whatever you may have heard about me—that you hold so false an opinion of my honor."

A mother would not raise her eyes to a son lost and believed dead in battle with more joy and wonder than this Saracen felt when she appeared to him so suddenly, in all her pride and grace and angelic beauty. Full of sweet desire, he moved to her, his lady, his goddess, and she threw her arms around his neck and held him tight for a moment. She had never gone so far when he was fighting for her in Albracca, in Cathay. Now she saw in him the sudden promise of seeing her own land again, and soon.

And she gave him a complete account of events from the day she had sent him to request aid for Albracca from the King of Sericana and Nabatea. She told him how Orlando had kept her from death, dishonor and all evil, and how her virgin flower was preserved, untouched as in her mother's womb.

Maybe this was true—if not believable to a man in his full senses. But it was easy for Sacripante to believe it; he had lost his way in a deeper error—love. Love can make what a man sees invisible to him, and Love can make him see things that are in truth invisible. Sacripante believed her because he wanted to. And it was true enough that she did not love Orlando. She did not tell Sacripante—any more than she had told Orlando—that she had come back to France only in order to find Rinaldo. That, anyway, no longer mattered, because she had drunk from the Fountain of Disdain in the Ardennes wood.

Sacripante, believing her, was meanwhile saying to himself, "If Orlando—the idiot—did not know enough to seize his good fortune, the loss is his. Fortune may smile but once. I will not follow his bad example. I will not let go the chance that is given me, and then be sorry for myself again. I shall pluck the rose—fresh, in the morning—for if I leave it any longer I may lose it—overripe, overblown. I know very well that you can't do anything with a woman more sweet and pleasing to her, however scornful she may pretend to be about it before, however sad she may be afterwards, for a while. I am going to pluck the rose, and I will not be put off by any pretense or protest."

But while he planned and prepared the sweet assault on Angelica, who did not suspect it, they heard a great noise from the nearby woods. Most unwillingly, he angrily gave up the plan, put on his helmet, went to his destrier, bridled him, mounted and took up his lance.

Out of the wood rode a knight who seemed strong and brave. His surcoat was white as snow, and a pure white streamer flew from the crest of his helmet— showing, Sacripante thought, that he was newly knighted. The king could not tolerate this interruption of his pleasure. He confronted the unknown knight with an evil—or guilty—look, and challenged him to fight, sure of his own ability to knock him out of the saddle.

The knight cut short Sacripante's threats, spurring at once and lowering his lance to the rest. Sacripante wheeled about in a rage and they rushed with leveled lances straight at each other.

Fighting lions or bulls do not leap at each other so fiercely as these two warriors rode. Each spear passed through the opposing shield. The encounter made the woods resound, from the grassy dale where they met to the rocky hilltops on either side, and it was good that both their breastplates held behind their pierced shields. Neither steed shied, either. They butted like rams. Sacripante's did not survive the blow, but died almost immediately. The other horse also fell, but was quickly revived by the spurs in his sides, while

Sacripante's remained lying on its master with all its dead weight.

The unknown champion, upright and seeing the other on the ground under his horse, decided he had had enough of that combat and did not care to renew it. He rode away at full speed through the trees; and before Sacripante had freed himself (with Angelica's help) the white knight was almost a mile away.

Like a stunned and stupefied ploughman after a thunderbolt has just knocked him flat, climbing to his feet, seeing his cattle dead all around him, and trees without their green crowns—so Sacripante got up after his fall. He especially regretted Angelica's being there to see the unfortunate accident. He sighed and moaned, not on account of bruises, dislocations or fractures, but purely on account of shame—shame greater than any he had ever felt before or would again. Moreover, besides being overthrown, his lady had had to help him get out from under his expensive dead horse. He would have remained speechless forever, I think, if she had not helped him in that, too, and given him his voice again.

"Oh, my lord," she said, "don't be too sorry about this! Because the fall wasn't your fault, after all, but the horse's. He needed rest and refreshment, not jousting. And that other knight has not added to his own glory. He was the loser, because he did not wait. That proves it. If I know anything about these things, I know that whoever first quits the field is the loser."

While she was comforting him, a messenger with horn and pouch galloped up, looking tense and tired, on a worn-out horse. When he reached them, he asked Sacripante if he had seen a warrior with a white shield and streamer pass by.

"As you see," said Sacripante, "he has just overthrown me, and he went that way, just now; and so

that I shall know again whomever it was who unhorsed
me, let me know his name."

"What you ask me," the messenger told him, "I will
answer immediately. Know, then, that you were
knocked from your saddle by the noble valor of no
man, but by that of a gentle damsel. She is brave, and
even more fair than brave. Neither do I hide from you
her famous name: it was Bradamante, the daughter of
Duke Aimone, Rinaldo's sister, who has taken away
from you, sir, whatever glory you may have earned in
this world."

With which, he loosed the reins, spurred and rode
on, leaving the Saracen unamused, not knowing what
to say or do, burning with humiliation. He could not
bear it—not only felled, but felled by a woman! Mounting Angelica's poor palfrey, he pulled her up behind
him without a word—postponing more pleasant pas-
times for a more peaceful place.

They had not gone two miles before they heard
the surrounding woods in another uproar, and soon
a great destrier appeared—richly adorned, equipped
with gold, but riderless and leaping or crashing through
everything in his way.

"If the gloom and all these tangled branches don't
deceive me," said the lady, "that horse ploughing
through the middle of the forest where there is no
path is Baiardo—I'm sure it is Baiardo. I know him.
Oh, how well he sees what we need! He's coming to
me! He knows that one spent horse is not enough for
the two of us, and he is coming to help."

Sacripante of Circassia dismounted and approached
Baiardo, intending to take the reins in his hand. Baiardo
responded by turning and kicking like lightning, but
the blow did not hit Sacripante. Unhappy the man who
feels those hoofs—for Baiardo could kick hard enough

to crack a great mass of metal, a metal hill, not just metal armor.

Then the great beast went tamely to Angelica, as happy as a dog greeting a master who has been away for days. Baiardo still remembered how she had served him with her own hands in Albracca—the time when she was in love with his master Rinaldo, when Rinaldo was so cruel and ungrateful to her. She took the bridle with her left hand, and stroked his neck and his chest with the other. The steed—who had extraordinary intelligence—quieted down like a lamb.

Sacripante seized the opportune moment; he mounted Baiardo and held on tight. The damsel returned to her own poor palfrey.

Then, turning, she saw that tireless knight who walked, resounding in his armor, through the wood behind Baiardo—after Baiardo, and after her. All her new hatred took fire again when she recognized Rinaldo. He now loved and desired her more than life; she hated him and fled like a dove from a falcon. There had been a time when he hated her more than death and she loved and desired him; chance had now changed their roles.

For this love and hate was caused by two springs of water of different effect not far from each other in the forest of Ardennes. One fills the heart with love. Whoever drinks from the other one is left without love—all ardor turned to ice. The one was a natural spring; the other, a fountain made by Merlin for lovers in anguish. Rinaldo had drunk deep from the one, and coming upon Angelica as she returned from the East, had on the instant been melted by love of her. But she in that moment was just drinking from the other, whereupon the love for him that had brought her back across the world turned to swift and automatic loathing. This latest sight of him menaced her again with fear. Her clear eyes darkened, and with trembling voice and tormented expression she implored Sacripante not to wait for the approaching knight but to escape with her.

"Am I then," asked the Saracen, "am I then so discredited in your eyes that you consider me useless? Not good enough to defend you from that fellow? Have you already forgotten the battles of Albracca? And the night when I, alone and naked against Agricane and all his host, shielded and saved you?"

She did not answer. She had no answer. Rinaldo was by this time too close, already threatening the Saracen, as he saw the horse—his own, indeed—and the lady whom he proposed to make his own.

What happened next between these two proud knights, I reserve for the next chapter.

TWO

The Castle of Iron

O Love, most unjust god, why do you so rarely let human desires coincide? Why, O treacherous god, do you take your pleasure in mismatching us so often? You will not let me cross the clear, easy ford, but drag me in where the water is deep and dark. You do not let me want the one who wants me, or make the one I want, want me: I find love only where I do not want to find it; and I must worship one who hates me. . . .

And you made Angelica look ravishing to Rinaldo when to her he seemed altogether repulsive. When he appeared beautiful to her, and she loved him, he hated her with all his being. Now he suffered, he tortured himself in vain—repaid in the same coin. She hated him; hated him so much that she would rather have death than him.

Running toward them, Rinaldo was shouting in a rage of pride, "Thief, get off my horse! I don't let anybody take what's mine. I make anybody who tries pay dearly. I will take this lady, too. It would be a big mistake to leave her to you. A perfect steed, and a lady worth so much, for a thief! Thief, you don't deserve them!"

"You lie when you call me a thief," the Saracen answered, just as proudly. "I could call you a thief with much more truth, according to what they say about your taxes at Montalbano. But I'd rather prove that I am more worthy of having the lady and the horse—since

I agree with you that there is nothing worth more in all the world than this lady."

Like two ferocious dogs who stiffly circle each other, snarling and showing their sharp teeth, squinting with eyes red as coals, then are suddenly at each other's throats, snapping, so Sacripante of Circassia and Rinaldo of Clermont went from challenge and insult to fierce swordplay.

The one was on foot, the other mounted, but this did not give the Saracen any advantage; Baiardo was no more help to him—maybe less—than he would have been to an inexpert page or squire, because by natural instinct he refused to do his true master any harm. The Saracen could not manage him by spur or hand. When he meant to drive the horse, the beast stood still, and trotted when he should have stood steady. Finally he threw his head down and reared and kicked. Realizing that it would take a long time to break this proud animal, the Saracen put his hand on the saddle-bow, rose, and threw himself from the left side to the ground.

When he had jumped free of Baiardo's stubborn fury, a really ferocious battle began—the kind of battle that can only occur between two equally valiant and gentle knights. Their clashing swords rang high and low. The hammer of the god Vulcan, beating out the thunderbolts of Jupiter on his anvil in his smoky cavern, sounds in slower time than did either of those two swords.

Both were masters of the game; now lunging, now feinting; suddenly rising, crouching, covering themselves or leaving themselves a little open, advancing and giving way, turning to strike yet again and again. And where one gave an inch of ground, the other took it at once.

Finally, Rinaldo maneuvered to hold his sword Fusberta high over Sacripante, and when it came down,

he gave his all in the blow. Sacripante did manage to
present his shield; it was of thick bone, with well-
tempered steel plates. But Fusberta cut through, for all
its armored thickness. The tall trees all around shivered
from the sound of that blow. The bone and iron seemed
to turn to ice on the Saracen's arm, and the whole arm
went numb.

When the nervous lady saw the damage done by that
single blow, fear again distorted her lovely face. She
might have been a condemned felon with her last
moments at hand. She felt she could not wait an instant
longer, or she would be taken by that Rinaldo whom
she hated as much and as disconsolately as he loved her.
Turning her palfrey, she drove him down a rough and
narrow path in the thick woods, often looking back, pale
and wan with fear—for it seemed to her that Rinaldo
was close behind even while she still heard the battle.
And when she could hear it no more, she was even
more afraid.

But she had not fled very far this time before she met
a hermit in a dismal valley. He was riding slowly toward
her on a donkey. He had a long, white beard and he
looked devout and venerable—wasted away by many
years and much fasting and, apparently, as shy and
scrupulous of conscience as anyone ever could be. As
he made out the delicate features of the damsel who
rode up to him, he was touched, moved, indeed excited,
by charity.

She told him her troubles and asked him if he could
guide her to a seaport, because she wanted to get
away from France and never hear of Rinaldo—not so
much as his name—again.

And the friar, who knew magic, eagerly comforted
the lady, promising her that soon he would deliver her
from all evil. He reached into his pouch, took out a
book, and exhibited some of its magic power. For he

had not finished reading the first leaf he turned to, muttering in his beard, when a spirit came forth in the shape of a squire. And when it appeared, he commanded it to do his will.

Compelled by the power of the book, the thing went right to the place in the wood where the two knights faced each other—not resting in the shade, but still fighting on, though exhausted. And it boldly stepped between them.

"Please," it said, "will one of you show me what good it will do the winner, when he kills the other one? When the battle between you is finally over, what will you—one of you—have, for all his exertion, if Count Orlando of Anglante, without a word or a stroke of his sword, without having broken so much as a single link of mail, conducts the lady who caused your fell combat to Paris?

"My lords, I met Orlando only a mile away—Orlando and Angelica! He is headed for Paris with her, and they were laughing at you together, making fun of your fruitless dispute. Perhaps it would be better for you at this point, while they are not yet too far, to follow their trail. For if Orlando is able to get her to Paris, you might never see her again."

Then, my lord reader, you would have seen the two knights discouraged and dismayed by this announcement, telling themselves how blind and stupid they were to let their rival mock them and scorn them like that.

Good Rinaldo marched to his horse Baiardo, panting and swearing in frenzied hate that if he got to Orlando he would cut out his heart. He flung himself on Baiardo's back and galloped away. He did not say good-bye to the king he left afoot in the woods, much less invite him to ride on the croup. And the brave horse, urged on furiously by his master, cleared or crashed through everything in the way—ravines, rocks, thorn bushes, streams—to Paris.

I don't want it to seem strange, my lord, that Rinaldo so quickly took the horse he had chased in vain for days, and so easily handled him after he took him. Baiardo, who had near-human intelligence, had not disobeyed through bad habit or perversity, but in order to lead him—all those miles—to the lady he knew his master now longed for. When she fled from the pavilion on the battlefield, Baiardo saw and followed her—his saddle happened to be empty at that moment because Rinaldo had dismounted in order to fight on equal terms with a knight of equal, or maybe superior, skill. Baiardo had then trailed Angelica from a distance through all her wanderings, guiding his master toward her. He was not willing to let Rinaldo climb into the saddle earlier, because then he would have had to obey him—and probably go the wrong way. And on account of the sagacious beast, Rinaldo did indeed find her twice, though he did not catch her—prevented first by Ferrau, then, as you have also heard, by Sacripante.

Now, equally believing the demon who gave Rinaldo false news of her, Baiardo dutifully obeyed as usual. Rinaldo, hot with love and wrath, drove him at full speed and always toward Paris; and he flew as fast as he could; but however fast he flew, any horse—or even the wind—would have seemed too slow to Rinaldo.

That night Rinaldo did let him rest, though it troubled him to give up chasing his cousin, the great lord of Anglante—since he still fully believed the false story given by the false messenger sent by the false friar, that sly magician. But he rode until late in the evening, and rode on early in the morning, and all that day he rode until he came to the city, where Charlemagne had retreated with the broken remnant of his host.

Because Charlemagne expected more battles, and probable siege, from the King of Africa, he was retrenching there, diligently gathering in more men and provisions, cleaning the ditches and moats and repairing the walls of Paris, doing anything and everything for its defense without delay, and he was just thinking of sending to England to call for more men, to form a new army. He did not want only to prepare Paris. He also hoped to march into the field and try the fortunes of open warfare once again, before he was besieged.

So as soon as he saw Rinaldo he dispatched him to Britain (as England was called in those days). The paladin objected very strongly to going, not that he had anything against that country, but because his Uncle Charles made him go right away. He never did anything less willingly. He was not left one day, not one hour, to hunt for Orlando and Angelica. Nevertheless, he obeyed the king, rode on and found himself at Calais in a few hours, and embarked for Britain the very same day.

Being so eager to reach Britain and get back, and against the advice of every pilot in the port, he had the ship set sail at a bad time, with a big storm threatening and the waves already rough. The threat was carried out; the Wind, enraged by man's arrogance, raised the waves with such fury that they were soon as high as the crow's nest. The anxious sailors lowered the larger sails, intending to turn back to port.

"That doesnt satisfy me," said the Wind. "I do not care to tolerate the liberty you have taken."

And it blew and bawled and threatened shipwreck if they turned any way except on the course the storm itself set for them.

Now astern, now against the bow, it raged mercilessly and never subsided but always increased; the ship turned here and there, scouring the high sea with low sails, helpless.

But because I have to weave various threads in an intricate plot in order to cover everything I intend to tell you, I must leave Rinaldo in the storm-tossed prow and turn to speak of his sister, Bradamante. You remember her: that famous young lady paladin who unhorsed King Sacripante not long before Rinaldo caught him on Baiardo. Bradamante was a sister worthy of Rinaldo—a daughter worthy of the great Duke Aimone of Clermont, and of Beatrice, his good wife. Bradamante's great strength and courage pleased Charlemagne and all of France as much as did Rinaldo's.

Bradamante was also loved by Ruggiero, a knight who had come out of Africa with his king, Agramante. He was a pagan, but he had his name from his father, Ruggiero of Reggio. That Ruggiero had loved Galaciella, daughter of the then King of Africa, Agolante. Her brothers, the cruel Almonte and Troiano, had driven her out into the desert to bear a child and die. Now Ruggiero her son, reared by the Moorish magician Atlante, was the pride and hope of Agramante's invading army.

Bradamante, who was not hardhearted, did not scorn such a lover. Indeed, she loved him, although Fortune had not been kind to them and they had seen and talked with each other only once. Then the war that brought them together separated them again. Afterwards, she went looking for him—as safe unaccompanied as if she had an army to escort her. And after she overthrew the King of Circassia, she crossed the forest, and after the forest she crossed a mountain, arriving at last at a beautiful spring in a meadow in the hills.

The spring rose in the middle of the meadow, and its

stream meandered about old trees that cast wide shadows over the water, so that the murmuring shade invited every passerby to stay and rest. A cultivated hill on the left now kept off the midday heat. As soon as her clear eyes took it all in, the girl noticed a knight— a knight in the shadow of a grove on the green bank among white, red and yellow flowers, sitting alone, thoughtful and still beside the glassy water. His shield and helmet hung from a beech-tree nearby, where his horse was tied. He looked up when he heard her riding toward him. He was crying miserably.

Brandamante, moved by the curiosity we all feel for news of others' troubles, and indeed, moved by his dispirited aspect, asked him the reason for his sorrow. Touched by her courteous speech and her noble appearance, for it was obvious at first sight that she was a strong and brave warrior, he told her the whole story.

"Sir," he began, "I was leading footmen and cavalry toward the camp where Charlemagne was waiting for Marsilio of Spain, to catch him when he came down from the mountains, and I happened to have a very lovely lady with me with whom I was fervently in love, and near the city of Rodenna I encountered someone— something—in armor riding a huge, flying steed.

"As soon as this thief—whether mortal, or one of those obnoxious infernal spirits—saw that dear girl of mine, he swooped like a falcon—down and up high again in an instant—and reaching out, he caught her and took her with him. I was not even aware of this attack until I heard her screams from high overhead. It was like the greedy kite's falling on the poor chick, near the hen who can only regret her carelessness and call and cluck after it in vain. I can't chase a man who flies up among the mountain peaks—I have an exhausted horse who can hardly pick his way along the rough, stony paths up there.

"But because I would have cared less—less, I say! —to see my heart torn from my breast than to lose her like that, I let my men go on their way without a leader, and without any guide I took the way Love showed me—in the direction it seemed the rapacious devil had carried my comfort and my peace.

"Six days I went on, morning to evening, through the dreadful mountains, by steep slopes and sheer cliffs where there is no road, no footpath even, and no sign or trace of man. Then I arrived at a rough, wild crater-valley, walled by cliffs, scored by gorges, pocked with terrible caves. There, in the midst of desolation, a high rock, and on its summit a castle, well situated and strong and wonderfully fair.

"From far off, it looks like fire. It is not built of brick or stone. And as I came closer to those splendid walls, the work looked ever finer and more marvelous to me. I learned afterwards that industrious demons, dragged up from below by strange fumigations and by sacred words put into infernal verses, have walled the whole place with iron. That iron was tempered in the Stygian waves and flames, deep in the Earth. Each metal tower is polished like a sword blade, and all the walls are smooth and bright as a mirror, so the surface never rusts or stains.

"The wicked robber raids all the country around, day and night, and drags his loot to that eyrie. Nothing is safe from him if he wants to take it. No one can stop him, only curse or raise a clamor after he's gone. And there he holds my lady, my heart itself, and I have lost every hope of recovering either.

"Alas! What could I do except watch the far-off fortress where my love is hidden away? Like the fox who hears the cub crying in the eagles' nest, and runs about below not knowing what it can do without wings. That rock is so steep, the castle so high, that no one can get up to it who cannot fly.

"While I lingered, watching, two knights arrived there, guided by a dwarf. They gave me some hope, besides my vain desire, but the hope was just as vain. Both of these warriors were of the highest valor: one was Gradasso, the famous King of Serican, who came to France some years ago to capture Rinaldo's horse and take Orlando's sword, and although he has failed, you know, he is generally believed to be otherwise invincible; and the other was a bold, strong youth named Ruggiero, who is very much admired in the African court.

" 'They come,' the dwarf told me when I asked, 'to try their strength against the lord of the iron castle, who, in a hitherto unheard-of new fashion, rides, armed and in armor, the huge, winged quadruped or four-legged bird.'

" 'O lords,' I said to those pagans, 'pray be moved by pity for my evil fortune and when, as I hope, you conquer, I beg you to restore my lady to me!' And I told them how she had been taken, with my tears affirming my sincere sorrow.

"They sympathized and assured me they would help, and then they went down the dreadful slope. From on high, I watched the battle closely, praying to God for their victory. Below the castle is a plain about two stones' throw across. When they got there, at the foot of the rock, they decided which one of them would fight first. Either because Gradasso drew the lot, or because young Ruggiero did not care to dispute his precedence, it was the King of Serican who raised his horn to his mouth. The sound reverberated from the stone wall and the iron wall surmounting it.

"And behold, out of the gateway high above, appeared the knight, fully armed and on the winged horse!

"It took off little by little, like the pilgrim crane, who runs first, rises a slow yard or two, then spreads his wings wide and soars so high, so fast. So the magician mounted to a height I think the eagles hardly ever dare.

"And then, when he was so minded, he had the steed fold wings and fall straight and fast as lead out of the sky, like a trained falcon after a duck or dove close to the ground. With his lance in the rest he came cleaving the air with a terrifying scream. Gradasso scarcely realized he was the target before he was hit. The magician broke his lance on Gradasso. And Gradasso, striking back, wounded the empty air, the wind of his passage, for the flier did not pause to deliver the blow and was already far away again. Gradasso has, or had, an Alfana, the most beautiful and best that ever wore a saddle. That grave encounter made the sturdy horse fall back on the plain.

"Once again the flier ascended to the stars. He spiraled round and returned, diving even faster, and this time it was Ruggiero he hit—Ruggiero, who did not even know he was coming down again, intent as he was on Gradasso, who was still recovering. Ruggiero bent from the heavy blow and his horse recoiled a pace though it did not fall, and when Ruggiero was ready to strike back, he saw the attacker up in the sky again— a speck only, he was so high.

"And so it went. Now he hit Gradasso, now Ruggiero—on the head, the breast, the back—while their own blows were empty, cheated by his speed. He would go gyrating around in tight or spacious circles, and when he seemed to aim at one he hit the other, dizzying their eyes in his rapid flight so that they could not gauge his direction.

"And they choked in the dust whipped up by his courser's giant wings.

"The battle between the two warriors of the earth and the one from the sky lasted until the hour that spreads over all the world that dark veil that discolors and obscures all fair things. And then . . .

"Now, what I say is true, and I don't exaggerate at all. I saw it. I know. But it still takes courage to tell anyone, because this last wonder sounds more like fiction than truth. But it is true.

"This knight of the heavens had kept the shield on his arm covered up, all this while, in rich silk. I don't know why he spent so much time, like a cat with mice, before he uncovered it. For the moment he does so, and shows the shield openly, it has such power that whoever sees it is left dazzled, stunned, falling like a corpse, utterly helpless under its magic spell! The whole shield shines by itself like a giant ruby, or even brighter; there can be no other light so strong. You have to fall before that splendor, blind and unconscious.

"I, too, even so far away, lost my senses, and only much later did I finally revive, to see neither one of the warriors, nor that dwarf, any longer; only the field below, empty, dark, and the castle above glittering with starlight; nothing else, save quiet.

"I concluded that the enchanter had taken both of them at once by the power of the shield's light, and had them captive inside. So they lost their freedom and I my last hope. I said my parting words to that place which held my heart, and I came away. Now judge if any other cruelty inflicted by Love can equal mine."

When the knight had told Bradamante the reason for his grief, he fell silent, as he had been when she found him.

She could not know that he was Count Pinabello, son of Anselmo of Altaripa, of the evil House of Maganza. The whole family was wicked. And never having wanted to be its only loyal and honest member, Pinabello did not merely conform to their abominably corrupt standards, but surpassed them all in vice and depravity.

But Bradamante did not think to ask him his name; she thought only of Ruggiero. She stood quietly listening to this unknown Maganzese with, as you would imagine, varying emotions and expressions. The first time she heard the name Ruggiero, her face glowed with more joy than ever; but when she heard that he was in imminent danger, it paled with pity. And she was not satisfied with one or two tellings of the tale, but asked the knight to go again over those parts most important to her. When she let him be done, and everything was all only too clear to her, her lovely face was still again. But she was not resigned to the situation, though it sounded impossible to correct.

"Knight, rest assured," she said to him. "It was lucky that I found you, today. Let us go at once to that citadel of avarice that holds hidden so rich a treasure. None of your trouble will be wasted, unless Fortune has become my implacable enemy."

The knight responded by asking, "Do you really want me to retrace all my steps through the mountains, in order to show you the way? Ah, well, it doesn't matter much to me to lose the time and effort, having lost everything else. But you, for all your pains, will go—over all that wasteland, all cliffs and gorges—to prison. Well, so be it. But you will have no reason to blame me, because I've warned you and you are willing to go nevertheless."

"I am eager to go," she said.

So he went back to his horse and mounted, to guide the brave young lady, who was willing to go not only to prison but to her death in order to save Ruggiero from the master of the iron castle.

As they set out, a messenger rode up behind, yelling,

"Wait! Wait!" at the top of his voice; that same messenger who let Sacripante know that it was she who had sent him sprawling on the grass in the woods.

And he brought news to Bradamante of Narbonne and Montpelier—how they had raised the standard of Marsilio of Castile, with all the coast of Acquamorte—and also how her city Marseilles despaired of defending itself in her absence, and sent this message, asking for advice and aid against Spain and the traitors in France. This city and all the land around it for many, many miles—all the land that lies by the sea between the Var and the Rhone—had been given to Bradamante by the Emperor, who had such great faith in her because he was used to watching her valor and success in joust after joust at his tournaments. Now, as I said, that messenger had come from Marseilles for her help.

The girl was for a moment undecided, not sure whether she ought to go back at once, or go on to the iron citadel first. On the one hand, she weighed duty and honor; on the other, her love. Her love tipped the balance. She decided to persist in the present quest to free Ruggiero from the magic castle. If her strength could not prevail against the magic, she might at least survive, to remain a prisoner beside him. So she put the messenger off with some excuse that seemed to satisfy him for the time being. Then she pulled on the bridle, turning her horse to resume the journey she had just begun with Pinabello—who seemed somewhat less than happy about it.

He knew now that she was of Clermont, the line and house that he and his hated publicly, and hated even more in private. And he imagined he would be in trouble if she knew him for a Maganzese. She was his natural, hereditary foe. Between the houses of Maganza and Clermont there was old, intense hatred, and they had broken the peace many times over many years, spilling rivers of blood. In his heart, therefore, the evil count decided to betray the unwary girl, or at least, as soon as the opportunity arose, to leave her alone in the mountains and take another road. And he became so preoccupied with his inborn hate and his present distrust and fear that inadvertently he lost his way and found himself in a dark, thick forest pierced, not too far ahead, by a high hill with a summit of naked rock. And the daughter of Duke Aimone of Clermont never left him; she was still there, right behind.

This, thought the Maganzese, looking about the tangled woods, is where he might shake the girl off.

"Before it gets any darker," he said, "it would be best to head for a night's lodging. Beyond that peak, if I recognize it, down in a valley, there's a rich mansion. You wait for me here, while I climb the hill to make sure."

Whereupon, he drove his tired horse toward the solitary hill, on the lookout for some point where he could sneak away and shake her from his trail. When he had driven the animal up beyond most of the treetops, he noticed a shaft or mine in the rock still higher above the path. He dismounted, climbed up, and peered down into it. The shaft, he judged, was over thirty yards deep. The stone had been cut with picks and chisels on all sides, descending smooth and sheer to a turning, or a small, square cell with an open gateway on one side— right into the heart of the mountain. Evidently the gate gave access to a larger, deeper cave. You could tell by the light that streamed out, as if a torch burned in the hollow heart of that strange peak in the forest, or as if the place beyond were the lip of the mouth of Hell. Pinabello had only a moment to stand there on the brink before the girl he dreaded overtook him. She rode lightly up the hill, having followed for fear of losing her guide.

Then that traitor saw that he could not simply leave her behind, and his evil fear helped him invent a strange, new means of disposing of her, or of dispatching her.

He went down to meet her and made her dismount and climb back up on foot, in order to show her where the rock was pierced and hollowed out; and he said he had seen a young lady with a smiling face at the bottom of the well—a young lady, he said, who by her pretty looks and costly gown seemed to be of no ignoble status, but who seemed displeased to be imprisoned down there. Bradamante looked down of course, and saw nothing but the bare stone in the weird light. But he told her that was because no sooner had he begun to ask the lady about her predicament than he saw someone pounce out of the inner cavern and in a frenzy force her back inside.

Bradamante, who was as incautious as she was brave, believed Pinabello and wanted to help the lady. Wondering, even before he had finished his lie, how she could set foot on the bottom, she looked around and saw the long branch of an elm tree whose leafy crown rose higher than most of the other trees of the forest. She quickly reached for it and cut it off with her sword. Then she let it down into the shaft. Entrusting the cut end to Pinabello, she grasped it lower down and slid over the edge of the pit.

Pinabello smiled and asked her how good she was at the high jump. Then he opened—and spread—his hands. And as she fell he called after her, "I wish I could bury all your people with you, here! All together! And wipe out your whole race!"

But the innocent girl did not meet the fate he intended, because, scraping and tumbling down the rock wall, the strong, firm branch of elm happened to crash at the bottom before her. Though it splintered, it sustained her enough to save her from death. But she did lie unconscious for a long time.

I shall attend to her, there, in the next chapter.

THREE

The Tomb of Merlin

Who will give me the words that the nobility of my next subject calls for? Who will lend my pen wings to help me reach the height of my theme? I need much brighter inspiration now than I am used to in order to fire my mind—for this part of my work I especially owe to my master; it is of his forefathers that I here have to write.

O Apollo, who shines on all the great globe of the world, you will never see (if the prophetic light that inspires me does not err), among all the illustrious lords allotted by Heaven to govern the Earth, a lineage more glorious in either peace or war as long as the celestial spheres revolve around the poles!

For this reason, writing of all its honor and fame would require not my pen but your lyre, Apollo—the lyre with which you gave thanks to Jupiter, the new ruler of the world, after he put down the furious rage of the Titans.

Or, if you ever lend me a better instrument, Apollo— one more fit to carve such precious stone as the beautiful images of the Estensi call for—I promise to put all my labor and talent into the task. In the meantime, I can but hack away crudely with my own incompetent chisel. Maybe later, with more diligent study of the art, I shall finish—and polish—the work to greater perfection.

First, we return to that traitor whose evil heart will not be protected by shields or by breastplates in the future: I refer to Pinabello of Maganza, who had hoped to kill the lady Bradamante. Thinking she was dead in the pit, and with a face pallid with fear, he left the scene of his crime. He scrambled down to his horse and remounted; and, as he had a twisted soul, he added crime on crime and led Bradamante's horse away with him.

Let him go. His attempt against another's life will assure his own death. And turn again to the lady who, betrayed by him, almost had her death and burial at one time in that one place.

But, as I've said, she did not die. She revived, though still bewildered from the impact of her fall on the hard stone at the bottom of the shaft. Getting up, she went through the open door that led into a second, enclosed, much larger cavern.

The room within, square and wide, appeared to be a venerable chapel. The weight of the peak above was sustained by thick columns of rare alabaster. An altar rose in the center of this room and a lamp burned in front of it. The clear, bright, steady flame illuminated the sanctuary and the cell outside, where she had fallen. Finding herself in a holy place, the girl was touched by devout humility and knelt before the altar and began to pray, thanking God for her life.

At that moment, a door in the wall behind the altar creaked and grated open and a woman appeared. Her robes and her hair were loose, and her feet were bare. She greeted the startled girl by name.

"O generous Bradamante," she said, "indeed you did not come here without divine consent. Many days ago, the spirit of Merlin predicted your arrival—unaware and unwillingly, by an unwonted way—to visit his holy remains."

"I did not know . . ."

"I know. But I knew. Merlin told me. And I am here

to welcome you, and to reveal to you what the stars have ordained for you, long, long ago. This is the ancient, famous, lost cavern that Merlin carved out for the Lady of the Lake. This is where she betrayed him and left him entombed, undead, under a spell. The crypt is below. There, to satisfy her whim, he lay down alive. And there he remains, his flesh corrupted, decayed, but with his soul still trapped in the corpse— trapped until the last day, when it will hear the angels' trumpets summon it to Heaven or send it to Hell like a dove or a raven. Which it will be, he does not know. But that is all he does not know, I believe. For his voice is still alive. You will soon hear how clearly it still speaks. Whoever asks him anything is answered freely and truly; he knows all past and future things.

"I came here, long ago, from a remote country in order to further my esoteric studies. Merlin is a great help, you understand. He mentioned your coming and named the very day you would arrive. See how accurate he is! This is the day! And I have waited here more than a month beyond the end of my course of study, because I wanted to meet you."

The daughter of Aimone was still frightened, but she stayed. She listened intently to the sorceress's speech, her heart so full of wonder that she was not sure whether she was sleeping or awake. And when the sorceress was done, Bradamante responded mildly and modestly, asking, "What have I to do with prophets, living or dead? Why do they bother to prophesy concerning me?"

The woman did not answer, whether she heard or not. She was back at the door she had opened, beckoning. Bradamante, now too interested to be afraid, followed her quickly. They went down into a brighter light, into the vault that entombed Merlin's soul along with his bones.

The great sarcophagus was cut from one huge block of hard stone, shining bright and clear as red flame. There was no other source of light in that place. Maybe there are some kinds of stone that naturally shine in the dark, like lamps. Or maybe this stone had been illuminated by magic fumigations and spells, or signs engraved according to astrological observations. A magical explanation of some sort would seem more probable to me. Anyway, the light of Merlin's sarcophagus filled that vault under the mountain, disclosing even more beautiful things all around; the entire tomb was decorated with sculpture and painting. Maybe Merlin was able to appreciate all that art.

Bradamante had no more than raised her foot over the threshold to the secret place when the live spirit in the decayed corpse of the magician spoke to her in a clear, living voice, saying, "May Fortune favor you and give you all you wish, O pure and noble virgin from whose womb will come a fruitful people whom Italy— and Germany and England and all the Earth—must honor. The ancient blood of Troy the Great, its two best streams joined in you, will produce the flower of all great families, the best the sun ever sees, from the Indus to the Tagus, from the Nile to the Danube, of all below the unnamed stars that shine over Antarctica and the stars you know, the constellation of Callisto, above the northern pole. From you and your children will come marquises, dukes and emperors, strong leaders who with wisdom and the sword will bring back to Italy all the ancient honor of invincible arms. Then just lords will wield the scepter, and, as under Numa Pompilius and Caesar Augustus, the Golden Age will come again under their benign good governing.

"And so that the will of Heaven be done, through you and through Ruggiero, who has chosen you—both of you having been chosen for each other from the beginning—bravely follow the path you choose. Let nothing stand in your way. Persist, so that you overthrow the thief who is keeping Ruggiero from you."

Merlin fell silent, having said all this in one breath, and gave the sorceress an opportunity to do her work; and she got ready to give Bradamante a preview of all her heirs. She had selected a great many spirits (whether from Hell or wherever, I know not), and she collected them all in that tomb, in diverse garb, with varied faces. Then she called the young lady back into the sanctuary, where she drew a circle that was big enough to contain her—even if she lay down with her arms stretched out—with a span left over. And so that Bradamante should not be harmed by the masquerading spirits, she gave her something to wear around her neck and told her to be still and only watch. Then she opened her book and called the demons.

And they all came into the cave from the shaft and gathered round the circle, where they were held back as though the sorceress and Bradamante were surrounded by a moat and a wall. Three times each shade of all that horde went round the circle, trying to get in, and then went into the crypt where the beautiful sarcophagus held the great prophet's bones. Not finding anyone to bother there, either, they went away, resuming their natural forms. But all the time they were in the sanctuary, around the circle, each one of them had the exact appearance of one of Bradamante's descendants.

"If I were to tell you the names and deeds of each one," said the sorceress, "that is, of the men who seem to be here with us, before their births, impersonated by these enchanted spirits, I do not know when we would be done. One night is not enough time to tell about so many. So I shall pick out a few for you, as many as may seem convenient, as time permits.

"You see that first one, who has your own good looks? He is to be head of your family in Italy. He will redden the earth with the blood of those Maganzese who betray and kill his father, and thus end the feud with them. He will also ruin Desidirius, who will thus be the last Lombard king to plague Italy. For this, the highest Emperor will give him dominion over Este and Calaon.

"The spirit behind him represents his son—your grandson—Uberto, who will defend the holy Chuch against the barbarians more than once. See, now, here's Alberto, invincible leader who will adorn so many shrines with trophies. Ugo the First, his son, is with him; Ugo will conquer Milan, crushing those serpents. That other one is Azzo, who will rule the Milanese afterwards. Behold Albertazzo, whose wise counsel will drive Beringarius and his son out of Italy. The emperor, Otho, will give him his daughter Alda in marriage.

"There's another Ugo, Albertazzo's son! Oh, what a beautiful succession!—its virtues undiluted! He will justly cure the Romans of their pride, and save the Pope from them, breaking their siege against him. And there's his brother Folco, who gives him his own rights in Italy and goes to rule Bavaria, saving the crumbling House of Saxony from collapse. He has Bavaria from his mother, Alda—and your line will maintain its rule."

The sorceress continued in this strain for several hours, through several hundreds of shades. At last she said, "Oh, I could go on forever! But now, as I told you before, if I had to show you every strong branch, every fair leaf of this exalted tree, it would take many nights and days. Now it seems to me it's time, if not past time, if it pleases you, that I stop talking and let the shades go."

Bradamante could only nod. The learned sorceress

closed her book. All the spirits still in the sanctuary dispersed and disappeared.

Here Bradamante, finally being given permission to speak, asked, "Who were the two sad spirits playing?— the ones we saw between Alfonso and Ippolito, at the end of the show? They sighed and looked as if all were lost, as if they had no pride or hope left in them. I noticed that those brilliant brothers seemed to shun them."

The enchantress's satisfied expression changed at that; tears fell from her eyes and she shouted, as if at the shades themselves, "Ah, miserable wretches! To how much pain evil men will lead you! And O good brothers, you worthy sons of Ercole the Good—do not let their sin overcome your kindness. They are still of your own blood. Let justice yield to pity in their case." Then she added, in a lower voice, "I won't tell you all about this. Not all of your descendants are wholly admirable, it's true. Those were the other two sons of Ercole. They will actually plot against their own brothers' lives, but luckily, Alfonso and Ippolito will find out in time. Don't let it embitter you.

"Now," she went briskly on, not giving Bradamante time to ask any more, "as soon as the sun rises in the sky, you will take the straightest way leading to the shining castle of iron, where Ruggiero lives in another's power. I will be your guide, until you are out of this wilderness. Then we will be at the sea, and I shall tell you how to go on, and what to do, so you will not be able to make any mistake."

The brave girl spent the whole night in Merlin's tomb, a good part of it spent talking with Merlin, who advised her to yield quickly to her Ruggiero, though this was advice she did not need. She fell asleep by his sarcophagus, and he woke her up in the morning, announcing that the sky was bright above the mountain, though the sun was not yet up. After a breakfast the sorceress somehow prepared, the two women left the hollow mountain by a secret tunnel, and then went down an immensely long path darkened and hidden by rocks and trees. It ended in a barren gorge amid inaccessible peaks, and for the rest of the day, without taking any rest, they climbed over boulders and cliffs and crossed the torrents that tumbled into the gorge and down it toward the sea.

But they made the going seem less tiresome and dangerous by pleasant chatter. Of course, most of it consisted of the older woman's advice and directions— which way to go, with whom, and what cunning Brada- mante must use if she still wanted Ruggiero.

"Even if," she said to Bradamante, "you were Pallas Athena or Mars, and even if you led more men than Charlemagne and King Agramante together, you would not be able to conquer or even resist the wizard who lives in the iron castle. Besides the fact that the im- pregnable rock is walled with iron, and so high; be- sides the way his steed goes galloping and leaping and diving and climbing in midair; besides these advantages, he also has the deadly shield. As soon as it is unveiled, its brilliance blinds the eyes and all the senses, and you are left like a corpse. You can't very well fight him with your eyes shut. How would you be able to know where he was, in order to dodge or strike? It's difficult enough with one's eyes open, even with eyes in the back of your head, on account of the flying steed. And I suppose the shield's light might pierce the eyelids anyway."

"Doesn't this mean," asked Bradamante, "that I can't fight him at all? Am I to be taken by him first, then? I am not Athena . . ."

"Athena couldn't fight him, either, I said. However, there is one way to escape the dazzling light and nullify all his other enchantments, too. It will be easy enough when I tell you, but it is the only way.

"King Agramante of Africa has a ring that was stolen from him in the East, from Angelica of Cathay, by Brunello—the world's best thief. It has power against all other magic; put it on your finger and you are safe from any spell. And Agramante needed it in order to make Ruggiero take part in his invasion. It was prophesied that Agramante would surely fail if he did not have Ruggiero's help, but Atlante the magician did not want to let Ruggiero join him. As you know, Ruggiero was freed, with this ring, and then he did indeed land with Agramante. But now he is trapped in the iron castle.

"And now Brunello once more has the ring, and is a few miles ahead of us, on his way to the castle, sent by his king to free Ruggiero again. He bragged that he could do it, and he promised his master he would. I suppose he can, the cunning fellow, with his wit and the ring. And Ruggiero is understandably dear to his master's heart.

"But it would be better if Ruggiero owes his escape from the magic trap to you, not to Agramante. So I will tell you how to go about it. You will go on for three days along the beach—for the sea is almost in sight, and we shall part. On the third day, you will come to an inn where the thief with the ring will be lingering —not eager to go on to the iron-capped rock. Oh, I almost forgot to tell you what he looks like. He is less than six spans tall. Black, curly hair. Dull, ashen skin, where not bearded. Puffy eyes with a shifty look. Flattened nose and bristly eyebrows. To complete the description, his clothes are tight and short, like a messenger's.

"You will meet him and happen to talk about magic. You will have to show your desire to go against the

magician in the mountains. But you must not let him
know that you have heard of the ring, or any such
defense against magic. He will offer to show you the
way as far as the valley of the rock where the iron
castle stands, and keep you company; he'll feel safer
himself, though he won't tell you he has to go there,
too, I am sure. Stay close behind him, and as soon
as you approach the place near enough to see it, kill
him. Do not let pity prevent you from following my
instructions at that point. And do it quickly, before he
can guess your intention and have time to use the ring
and escape. For that ring not only nullifies other magic,
you know; it has magic of its own; and if he has time
to put it to his mouth, he will disappear from your
sight. Then you would have trouble catching and killing
him, and he might kill you."

Their way thus accompanied by practical advice,
they came down to the sea near the mouth of the
Garonne, near Bordeaux. Here the lady magician and
the lady knight parted, with some tears.

Bradamante, who could not rest or think of resting
until she freed her lover from prison, traveled on, walking along the beach until, the next evening, she came
to the inn where Brunello had already arrived. She
recognized him as soon as she saw him, from the
description. She asked him where he came from and
where he was going. He answered her readily and lied
about everything. The lady, having been fully warned,
did not lie any less: she lied about her country, her race,
about her religion, her name, her sex. And while they
told each other all these lies, she often glanced covert-
ly at his hand and did not let him come too near her.
She could not help it; she could lie, but she could not
suppress her natural suspicion and simple dislike of a
man of his trade. She kept expecting him to disappear,
or pick her pocket, or both.

But while they stood together thus, their ears were suddenly deafened, their voices stopped for the moment, by a noise.

I'll tell you what made it, lord, after I have made due—or overdue—pause in the story.

FOUR

The Winged Horse of the Pyrenees

Although lying is subject to criticism, more often than not, and may indicate an evil mind, it has manifest benefits, too; it may avert embarrassment and bloodshed. We do not always talk with friends in this mortal life, which is more dark than bright and full of envy. If, after long experience, and at great cost, you may possibly find one person who is a real friend to whom you can openly speak your mind without any suspicion, how then would you expect Bradamante to behave with Brunello, who was neither innocent nor sincere but full of falsehood and pretense, as the sorceress had described him?

So she lied, too—lied as would be proper with the Father of Lies himself; and, as I said, watched his greedy, thievish hands the while. But his suspicions were not aroused. There was not time; there was a loud noise, outside.

The lady cried, "O glorious Mother, O King of Heaven, what is it?" and ran out of the inn.

There she saw the innkeeper and all his family, some at the windows and others out in the road, all with their eyes raised to the heavens as if there were an eclipse or a comet. But it was a rarer wonder; she saw on high something she would not easily have credited before: a great winged steed carrying a knight in armor through the air. The noise was the cry of the steed as it passed over the inn; out in the road, she still heard the thunder of its wings. Those wings were huge and wide and of varied coloring, and the knight sat between them—the feathered wings and the metal armor luminous in the lingering sunlight, high above, as the rider directed his path westward. The wonder rose up before the mountains, then plunged and seemed immersed among the dark peaks.

"That was the wizard," the innkeeper pointed out. "He makes the trip quite often, sometimes as near as that, sometimes farther. He can fly up among the stars, or just skim the ground; and he carries off all the good-looking women he can find, raiding the whole countryside so much that all the women who have good looks, or think they have, don't dare go outside in daylight. He steals all of them.

"He keeps a castle up there in the Pyrenees. It's made by magic, all metal, so bright and beautiful that I'm sure there's no other wonder in the whole world to match it. Of course many knights have gone there, but not one has come back to brag about it. He beats them all, and either snatches them up there, too, or kills them."

Bradamante was sure that with the anti-magic ring she could make the magician give up his castle and all its prisoners, and she told the host, "Now find me someone who would know the way to that place, because I can't wait to face this magician in a fair fight."

"You won't need to hire a guide," Brunello answered her, "if I may go with you. I have the route down in writing, and other things, and you will have nothing to worry about if you come with me." He almost mentioned the ring.

"I would be grateful for your company," she said, thinking that the ring would soon be hers. She said what was useful to say and kept quiet about whatever might hurt her with the little Saracen.

The innkeeper had a horse that satisfied her. It was

good for the road, and good for fighting, too. She bought it and set out as soon as the next morning's light appeared, up a narrow valley toward the sunlit peaks, with Brunello riding now ahead, now behind. Through fields and woods, over hills, into thinner woodlands and up more open, higher hills again, they eventually came to a place where the height reveals, if the air is clear, both France and Spain and both the Mediterranean and the Atlantic shores.

From there, they went down a rough, wearying road into a deep valley, and found a deeper one; a great rock rose in the middle of that barren place, and the summit of the rock was indeed encircled with a beautiful, mirrorlike wall of metal that rose so high that one had to look up to see the top, even from the outer ridges. Obviously the castle could be reached only by flight.

Brunello, not a little awed and cowed by the sight, said, "Behold where the wizard imprisons the knight— knights, and ladies."

The walls were straight and tall and the gate was high on the peak. The stone itself seemed to have been cut on all four sides perfectly—perpendicular as a good mason's plastered wall. On no side could they see a path or stair in the stone, much less in the metal. It was a good roost for a winged creature, a perfect prison for any other.

Here the lady knew it was past time to take the ring and kill Brunello. At the moment he did not have his mind on her, but on the castle, and he sat looking at it with his back to her. But it seemed vile to her to stain herself with the blood of an unarmed man, and one of such an ignoble sort, at that; and she thought she could get the ring without putting him to death, anyway.

She rode up beside him, picked him out of his saddle,

held him tightly, took the ring from his finger and tied him up. His tears, moans and lamentations did not move her; she left him tied to a branch on a high fir tree.

Then she went riding down the slope at a slow pace to the plain under the castle. From there, the whole castle on its high column of rock looked like a single tower, or a sword. In order to challenge the magician to battle she had recourse to her horn, and after the blast she shouted as loudly and fiercely as she could, summoning him to the field and daring him to combat.

The magician did not wait long before answering the call of her horn and her voice. The beak, the head and the neck of his steed appeared far, far above, the head cocked, eyeing her like a bird peering out of its nest in a tall tree. But there could be no bird as huge as this creature, and then the rest appeared, the cruel forelegs with their scales and claws, the shoulder of its folded wing, and peering over the edge of that, the wizard in armor. She saw the whole body of a great stallion then, as its powerful hind legs launched it into the air, for it was part griffin, but part horse. Its wings spread, its tail lashed, and it flapped down at her like a giant vulture.

But the lady paladin was relieved, from the beginning, to see that the magician carried no weapons. He had no lance or sword or mace to pierce or smash her armor. He had only his shield on his left arm. It was all covered with scarlet silk. And in his right hand he held only an open book. She could see the pages fluttering in the wind. As he flew, he read, his sole way of doing battle. He merely conjured up magic illusions; reading on the circling beast, he seemed to dive with a lance or swoop and swing a mace or short-sword. But he was actually still overhead and had not struck at all. All this was dazzling, or would have been if

Bradamante had not been wearing the ring she had stolen from the thief. As it was, only shadows seemed to fall toward her from the steed and rider and then return.

As for the steed, however, it was not feigned, but natural, got by a griffin on a mare. It had the feathers, wings, forelegs, head and beak of the griffin; the rest was wholly horselike. Such hybrids are called hippogriffs—natural, but very rare, found only in the Mountains of Rifei, in Hyperborea, beyond the frozen northern seas.

The magician had drawn this one from its homeland by magic incantations; and when he had it, he trained it rigorously, so that within a month it wore bridle and saddle. and he could make it walk, trot, run, take off and soar or hover in the air quite obediently. So this was not a magical fiction like all the rest, but true, and Bradamante could see that it was. But the battle was simulated. Magic can make white black and black white. But no illusions misled the lady knight, because she was wearing the ring.

Nevertheless, she cringed at the shadows that seemed to attack her, and she struck back at them, driving her horse here and there on the little plain, working hard and floundering about as if the battle were in earnest and desperate. And after some time at this exercise on horseback, she dismounted and pretended to fight on, meanwhile feigning great tiredness, and even fear. It was the way the sorceress had advised her to trap the sorcerer. If she had paid no attention to his mock battle, he would of course have been alarmed and might have withdrawn.

And then came the moment to work his direst magic, against which he neither knew of nor imagined any possible defense; still holding his open book on his high, hovering steed, he fumbled and clawed at the bright red silk and finally exposed the shield. He was sure that like anyone else this knight would fall before its magic splendor.

He could have uncovered it right away, of course, could in fact uncover it more easily from his inaccessible castle, without even coming out, and not hold each knight who came to conquer him at bay. But he liked to see them fight, he liked to see the lances fly and the swords swing, and he liked to impress people, too. So he played at battle until the fun turned to boredom, and only then prepared to take his victim.

She had watched him intently, especially after she dismounted. She had watched for this. And when he unveiled his shield, she closed her eyes almost completely and let herself fall to the ground. She heard her horse falling at the same time, not far away. The splendor of the gemlike shield did not bother her, though it still looked very bright; but she intended to lure the magician to the ground where she could reach him. A part of her plan that did not go wrong, either; for as soon as her head touched the ground, the hippogriff accelerated, swooped down in a tight circle and landed close by. She could hear its wings and feel their breeze as it passed right over; she could hear its hoofs strike the ground. She waited a moment, beginning to be afraid she would not hear the wizard when he came up to her, wondering if he might not simply stab her, thinking she must turn her head and look. But then she saw him coming slowly, half bent over from caution or from weakness—crablike, in his armor, over the yellowed grass. The hippogriff followed a few paces behind. The magician had left the shield, in its cover again, hanging on the saddlebow. He still carried the book he made war with, but closed, under his arm. He also carried a chain which he kept wrapped around his waist for tying up his victims. He came like some beast of prey; but she was waiting like one, too. He stood over her, bent down, let the book fall; his chain rattled against her armor.

She got up and threw him down.

He made no attempt to defend himself, and you can't blame him; he was a very feeble old man and she was much too strong for him.

Intending to take off his head, she raised her sword as soon as she had him down; but when she saw his face, she did not strike, scorning such easy revenge. She saw that he was a venerable ancient with a mournful face. From his wrinkles and white hair, she took him to be seventy years old at least. Actually, he was much older.

"Kill me, boy, for God's sake!" he said, full of spite and anger. But she was now more reluctant to take his life than he was to keep it. And she wanted to know who he was and why he had built the citadel in that savage place, to bother everybody.

"Not through evil intent, alas!" the wizard answered, weeping. "Not for evil reasons did I make that beautiful fortress on the summit, and it was not through greed that I became a robber; but only natural affection moved me to keep back, from a cruel end, a gentle knight. There was no other way to do it; for, as the stars prove, in a little while he would be obliged to die— and die a Christian—and die by treachery—if I let him go. And the sun does not shine, between the poles, upon a youth so good and fair. Ruggiero is his name. I, Atlante, have brought him up, ever since he was a little boy, sadly orphaned. Ambition for fame, together with his violent destiny, drew him to France with King Agramante. And I, who have always loved him as if he were my son, or more, sought to draw him back from France and his fate. I built the beautiful castle above only to keep Ruggiero safe. I caught him the same way I hoped to catch you today. And I collected the others, knights and ladies and other nobles, all the best people I could find, to give him some company so he would not be sad about not being able to go out. I ask nothing of them except that they stay. I take pains to give them everything else. All my guests can have as much of whatever they want under the sun. It is all there—music, singing, sports and games, vestments and viands, as much of everything as they want, just for the asking. So they are all happy, and he is happy, too. I took a great deal of trouble, and everything would have been fine, but your arrival ruins everything.

"Ah, if your heart is no less lovely than your face, do not interfere! Take the shield—I give it to you. It conquers everyone, except you, of course. Take the hippogriff—it sails through the air so fast! And do not meddle with my castle! Or take one or two friends of yours I might have there. Is that the trouble? And leave the rest. Or take them all, all the others. Oh, I ask nothing more, but leave me my little Ruggiero!"

But she was binding him with his own chain, and he must have read her intention in her eyes, for he went on, "Or if you mean to try to take him away from me, alas!—at least, before you take him back to France, please loose this afflicted soul from this henceforth rank and putrid husk!"

The young lady answered, "I will set him free. You must know that you're croaking nonsense. Don't offer me the shield as a bribe, or the steed, either. Both are mine now, not yours. Even if they were yours to give, the exchange you propose would not be a fair one, you know. You say you're keeping Ruggiero in order to prevent an evil end fixed by his stars. But either you cannot know what the stars ordain, or, knowing such things, you cannot avert them anyway. If you did not see your own fate today, when it was so near, you cannot very well truly foresee others'. No, don't ask me again to kill you. Your begging and weeping is all in vain. If you really want to die, even if everyone in the world should refuse to help you, you still could manage it yourself. But before you free your soul from your body, open the gate and let out all your prisoners."

While she was saying this, she was pulling him to his feet and pushing him toward the rock, not letting him go because she still did not trust him even though he seemed so mild and submissive. As she suspected, there was a way up, only hidden by magic, and on the far side: a cave that served as a stable, and stairs up one inner wall, then a fissure, then a tunnel winding back and forth until after a long climb they emerged beside the castle gate. The stone was solid, but she could see through the iron; and, because she was wearing the ring, could see the people inside the castle.

From the threshold, Atlante lifted a slab engraved with strange signs and characters. There were vases in the little hollow space underneath. They smoked continually from mysterious fires within. Atlante broke them and burst into tears again, and suddenly the flat summit of the rock was clear, desolate, with nothing on it but open air and people who were not as well dressed as they had thought. Neither wall nor tower appeared on any side. It was as if nothing had ever been built there; there were only some holes in the rock.

Atlante got away and scuttled into one of them, his chain clanking.

Bradamante did not follow him. She had eyes only for the crowd of bewildered people, only for the knights in the crowd, and only for Ruggiero—not that she could see him right away. She ignored the way some of the prisoners criticized her for giving them their liberty and depriving them of all their illusory (and, no doubt, licentious) pleasures. She looked for him.

There was Gradasso, there was Sacripante whom she had encountered before, there were Prasildo and Iroldo, those true friends who had come from Babylon with her brother Rinaldo. She did not recognize any of the ladies, or did not bother to recognize them. And at last she saw her long-desired Ruggiero.

"Did you do this?" he asked, throwing his arms around her, welcoming her warmly not for that alone; he had loved her more than his own life ever since the day she took off her helmet for him and was wounded. It would be too long a story to tell why, how and by whom—and then to tell how long these lovers wandered in the wild, lonely woods, searching for each other night and day, never seeing each other again after that first meeting—until now. Now that he saw her, and knew that she alone had redeemed him, his heart was so full of joy that he considered himself the luckiest and happiest man in the world.

Hand in hand, they made their way down the narrow, hidden stair to the valley at the base of the rock, where the lady had conquered the wizard. He led his horse, Frontino, from the cave, and outside they found Bradamante's horse and the hippogriff, too. The hippogriff was lying on the dry grass, with the covered shield still hanging on its saddle.

The lady went to take it by the reins, and it waited until she was near, its eagle eye on her warily. Just before she reached it, it heaved itself to its feet, simultaneously spreading its wings in the air, and flew off, only to alight again halfway up the hillside. Bradamante rode after it. As before, it flew away not high and not far, but like a crow leading a dog after it in the sand, now here, now there, idly, though it could quickly fly out of sight whenever it wanted to.

Ruggiero, Gradasso, Sacripante and those other knights she had freed also gave chase, running or riding after, or waiting where they hoped it might land to escape the others. It made them spread out all over the bottom of that strange valley—among the dry stone of the outer slopes, the yellow grass of the plain, the rock-filled, stagnant pools in the lowest places by the central peak. And once they were well distributed, with no one very near Ruggiero—not even Bradamante—it landed not far from him and stood still.

This was the work of old Atlante, who still had his pitiful hope of bringing Ruggiero out of all physical danger. He had no thought, no care in life but that. And so he directed the hippogriff in order to get him out of Europe and out of the war yet again.

Ruggiero caught the hippogriff and intended to lead it after him. But it stood still and would not follow. Ruggiero dismounted from his earthly steed and mounted the flying one. He spurred it lightly. It ran a short distance, then leaped like an ordinary horse—but it did not come down. Its wings were at work. It climbed the sky like a gyrfalcon whose master lifts off its hood, at the same time letting it see its prey almost directly above.

Bradamante had been hurrying toward Ruggiero. Seeing him so high, so quickly, in such danger, she simply stood in shock—and did not regain her full senses for some time. She could think only of Ganymede, caught in Troy, his native land, and carried up to Olympus by Jupiter in eagle form. She was afraid some god was taking Ruggiero, who was surely as beautiful as Ganymede—or any god. As for Atlante, even if he was still lurking on the summit—the hippogriff did not alight there. It went higher and ever higher. With her eyes fixed on the sky, she followed it as long as she could; when it was too far to be seen, her soul, her fears followed it still, for an uncounted span of time. She cried, and felt she would never stop crying until she saw Ruggiero again; she knew she would have no ease from pain until then.

Long after he was gone from her sight, she turned to his good destrier, Frontino, and decided not to leave him prey to anyone who might come along. Caressing him, she took his reins and led him after her. She would keep him and give him back to his master. She told herself now that she was sure to see him again.

The feathered courser flew on, and Ruggiero could do nothing with spurs or reins to control its flight. He could only look down and see Bradamante and the very valley he came from disappearing; the Pyrenees seemed to sink until he could not tell where the terrain was flat or rose or fell. And when the hippogriff had reached that great altitude, it took a course toward the place where the sun sets when it revolves in the constellation of Cancer: southwest. Soon Ruggiero saw no land below, but only the open Atlantic. And the hippogriff cleaved through the air fast as a sailboat with a greased hull and a stiff breeze blowing—or faster, and the flight was very smooth.

We leave him as he travels on so easily, and turn back to the paladin Rinaldo in the stormy sea with the angry wind that contested his effort to reach Britain.

All the next day and the day after, Rinaldo sailed on, though the canvas was low and torn, buffeted day and night hither and yon over the raging water, now westward and now toward the constellation of the Bear in the north.

At last, the shore of Scotland loomed before the ship. It was rocky and high and crowned with the Caledonian Wood, where one often heard the clash of swords among the ancient, shady oak trees. Knights errant went through that thick forest, the famous knights of all Britain, and also knights from countries near and far, from France, Scandinavia, Germany; those who were not very brave should not have gone there, or, hunting for fame, they were more likely to meet death. Great deeds were done there, in an earlier time, by Arthur, Lancelot, Tristan, Galahad, and other knights of the Round Table. Magnificent memorials and trophies remain to prove this, although they are lost and buried in those deep woods.

The ship was driven to cover on the rocky coast. It was not seriously damaged by the storm, but the wind still blew strong and unfavorable. Rinaldo took his arms, his armor and Baiardo, and quickly landed in the shadow of the overhanging trees. He ordered the pilot to put out to sea as soon as possible and sail on to wait for him at Berwick.

Then, without squire or any other company, the knight rode into that immense forest, taking now one path, now another, soon undeniably lost. At the end of the first day, he happened to come to a rich abbey, whose monks dispensed a good part of its property in honoring the knights and ladies who stopped there when wandering in the woods. They gave Rinaldo a hearty welcome, and after he had had his fill of their good food, he asked them if knights could still find strange adventures in that land, if it were still a place where a man could show, by doing notable deeds, whether he deserved blame or reward.

They told him that, roving those woods, he would be liable to find many strange adventures indeed, but that, like the place itself, the deeds done there tended to be misty and unknown.

"Try some place where your works would not remain obscure and buried, but become well known," they suggested, "so that Fame can follow your toil and your danger, and speak of them properly.

"And if you want to try your valor," they went on, "the worthiest deed ever done by a knight, whether in the old days, Arthur's age, or in modern times, needs doing; it's ready for you, or for another knight. The daughter of our king now stands in need of help. She must be defended against a baron named Lurcanio, who has ruined her reputation and is trying to take her life. This Lurcanio has accused her to her father, the king, maybe more out of hatred than for any other reason, of having committed fornication. He charges that she took a lover up on her balcony, in the middle of the night. By the law of the land, then, the princess is condemned to the stake, unless she finds a champion who, within a month, now already almost over, will prove that her accuser is lying. The hard law of Scotland pitilessly wills that any woman who couples with a man, unless she is his wife, of course, and is accused, and not defended, must die. There is no way to save her if some strong knight does not come, take up her defense, and prove that she's innocent and doesn't deserve to burn.

"The king, grieving for fair Ginevra (that's his daughter's name), has made it known throughout the realm that anyone, provided he's born of a noble family, who assumes her defense and disproves the libel will have her for his wife, and have rank and wealth, in a dowry suitable for such a maiden. But if no one comes for her in a month, or comes and does not beat Lurcanio, she will be killed.

"Such an enterprise would suit you better than random wandering through the woods. Apart from all the fame and honor, never to be taken from your name, you would win the flower of all the fair maidens from India to the Pillars of Hercules, for Ginevra is most fair, and wealth, and a realm, and the king's thanks for saving his all but extinguished honor. Besides, you are obligated by the laws of chivalry to avenge the treason done her, even if she were not a rich princess, because she is commonly believed to be a true paragon of chastity."

Rinaldo thought a while, outraged by their story, and then said, "So a girl must die because she let a lover prove his love? Damn whoever made that law! And damn whoever stands for it! A merciless woman may deserve to die, but not one who takes mercy on her true lover, and gives him life! Whether it's true or not that Ginevra let the man take her, I don't care. It's none of my concern. But I would praise her for having done it, if it were proven that she did.

"Don't look so dismayed," he went on. "I have turned every thought to her defense. I am determined to defend her. Just give me somebody to guide me quickly. Lead me to her accuser. I trust in God to deliver her. I don't want to say she didn't do it, for— not knowing—I might speak falsely. But I will say that there ought to be no punishment at all for such acts of love, and I will also say that whoever made that wicked law must have been out of his mind. I say that it ought to be repealed. It's easy enough to think up a more reasonable one.

"After all, if the same desire inclines—compels— both sexes toward that sweet end of love which some ignorant, common people may consider an excess or even a serious excess outside marriage (and I say it does compel them), why should they punish or even blame the woman for getting laid once or twice or however often with one lover or more, when the man can do it as often as he feels like it, and not only go unpunished, but be praised? The law is unequal, and therefore a clear injustice to all women, and I trust that God will let me prove in battle that it's a great evil and has been tolerated too long."

Rinaldo had the monks' complete agreement; all of them said that the law was ill-conceived and unjust and that it ought never to have been allowed, and some also said that the king who could correct it, but did not, did very ill indeed.

When the morning filled the eastern sky beyond the trees with colors from pure white to red, Rinaldo took up his arms, mounted his Baiardo, and with a squire lent by the abbey, started out on the long miles through the maliciously wild wood toward the place where the case was to be tried by arms.

Trying to shorten the great distance (for the squire's nag was slow), they had left the better way for a faint path, when they heard a scream that filled all the forest around them. It was not far off. The knight pushed Baiardo, the squire, his nag in the direction of the glen from which the scream had come.

There, between two cutthroats, Rinaldo saw a young lady who seemed pretty enough from that distance, but as tearful and terrified as anyone could be. She had good reason; the men beside her had drawn their swords and were about to strike and redden the grass with her blood. Her protests seemed to have made them hesitate. Then Rinaldo came riding down on them with a menacing cry far louder than her scream had been. Seeing help coming for her, and almost upon them, the killers quickly turned their backs and soon disappeared in the thick woods.

The paladin did not care to follow them. He rode to the lady and asked her what supposed crime of hers had attracted such punishment. Then the squire arrived, and to save time, Rinaldo had him lift her to the croup and then returned to the path.

Traveling on, getting a better look at her, he decided

that she was very beautiful, and also well-mannered, though she was still affected by the fear of death. Once she had calmed down, he asked her who it was who had planned to kill her, and why.

And she began, in a low, humble voice, to tell him what I intend to repeat in the next chapter.

FIVE

The Misfortunes of Dalinda

Of all the other animals on Earth, whether they live quietly and peacefully, or fight and make war, none of the males make war on the females. The female bear wanders safely in the forest with the male, the lioness lies down beside the lion, the female wolf is safe with the male, and the heifer is not afraid of the bull. What abominable pest, what Fury, then, possesses the human breast? For husbands and wives may scold each other with abuse and insults, and strike and bruise each other's faces, and shed not only tears, but sometimes blood, in senseless rage, in the bed they share. It seems to me that a man who is moved to hit a fair woman's face, or harm a hair on her head, commits not only a great crime, but one against Nature—and, therefore, a rebellion against God. But as for the man who gives a woman poison, or murders her with his bare hands, I do not believe that he can be called a man, but rather a spirit of Hell in human form. The two criminals Rinaldo drove away, who had dragged the girl into those darkly wooded glens so that no one would hear any more of her, must have been just such demons.

However, she was about to tell the paladin who saved her the cause of her sad fate. I shall therefore delay no longer in continuing her story.

"You will hear," the lady began, "of cruelty worse than ever could have been committed in Thebes or Argos or Mycenae, or in any other ancient, savage land.

And if the blessed sun, in his revolutions, does not come as close to this land as to others, I think that he must be reluctant to shine on such cruel people. That men may be cruel to their enemies, in any age, may be attested to by many examples; but to give death to one who always tries to be good to you is just too unfair, too impious. Well, in order to tell you the truth about why those beasts would have slaughtered me like that, in my youth, against all reason, I will tell you everything from the beginning.

"I want you to know, my lord, that when I was very young, I came to court to serve the king's daughter. I grew up with her, in an honorable position. Cruel Love, envying my happy state, made me his slave, made the Duke of Albany, of all the youths and knights I saw every day, seem most fair to me.

"And he seemed to love me very much, too, so I loved him with all my heart. Oh, you can hear what a man says, you can look in his eyes while he speaks, but you still cannot tell whether he means it in his heart. I believed him, I loved him, and I did not hesitate to go to bed with him. The first time, I didn't even consider where we were. It was in the princess's bedroom, where she keeps her very best things, and often sleeps. That room leads onto a balcony in the outer wall of the palace. My lover climbed up there. Then I hid a rope ladder in the room, and would let it down to him whenever I wanted him to join me. I had him come there as often as possible, whenever Ginevra was not there, because of course she changes rooms with the seasons; that place was best for the summer.

"His coming was never seen by anybody, because that wall of the palace faces some abandoned and half-ruined buildings where nobody goes by day or night. And our lovemaking went on for many days and months in secret. My love grew by the hour. It inflamed me so much that I felt all on fire inside. I couldn't do without it. And I was so blinded by it that I didn't see—didn't imagine—that he made love a great deal, and loved me little. I ought to have recognized his deceit in a thousand certain signs all along.

"But after some time he became a new suitor of Ginevra's. I don't know exactly when this began, after he became my lover, or even before. You see how arrogantly he ruled me, though; he told me about it himself, and didn't hesitate to ask me to help him win her. Of course, he did tell me it wasn't the same. He told me he didn't really love her, but only pretended to, and that he hoped to marry her lawfully. Getting permission from her father would be easy, if she herself were willing; for nobody in all the realm was of nobler blood or higher rank than he, except the king. He persuaded me that if I could help make him the king's son-in-law (for he simply had to be even closer to the king), I would be well rewarded and never forgotten; he convinced me that he would put me before his wife and all others and always be my love. I was concerned only in satisfying him. I didn't know—didn't want to know—how to oppose him; I couldn't imagine opposing him, and was happy only on days when I seemed to have pleased him.

"So I took every chance that came my way to talk about him, praising him to the skies. I spent all my time and skill trying to make Ginevra love my lover. I did everything I could, God knows; but I never had the slightest effect on her. I couldn't interest her in him at all.

"And this was because she had come to love, with all her heart and soul, a gentle knight, handsome and courteous, come to Scotland from a far country with a brother of his, when very young, to stay at our court. Here he became so perfect in arms that Britain does not hold a better knight. The king liked him, too, and showed it; he gave him castles and towns and domains of considerable value, and raised him up among the great barons. He was named Ariodante, by the way. And as the king marveled at his great valor, so did his daughter. Besides, she had learned that he loved her passionately. So she returned his love, with a true heart and perfect faith, and wouldn't listen to me. On the contrary, the more I begged and pleaded for my lover, the more she would criticize him or blame him for this or that.

"Meanwhile, I often encouraged him to give up his hopeless enterprise. I told him he couldn't hope to get her, because she was completely lost in another love. I told him plainly how she burned for Ariodante, and that all the waters of the seas could not quench the fire.

"Having heard this from me so often, Polinesso (that's the duke's name), who could see for himself that I was telling the truth, and how he displeased her with his love, at last couldn't stand it. He couldn't stand losing her, or her hand, nor could he stand seeing another preferred to him, since he was very proud. He took it so badly that his love—or pretended love—changed to a rage of spite.

"And he resolved to stir up so much hatred between Ginevra and her true lover that it could never be erased, and to put Ginevra in such disgrace that she never could clear her name, living or dead. But he didn't reveal his evil plan to me or anyone else.

"He only said to me, 'Dalinda (my name is Dalinda), you know how a tree can sprout again from its root, even when it has been cut down four or five times. In the same way, my stubborn pride, cut down by failure in this, cannot be killed. I must have what I want.'

"Well, I didn't know what he really wanted then, you know. 'I don't long for pleasure,' he explained, 'as much as for the proof that I could conquer, the feeling of conquest, at least. And, since I am not going to in fact—as you have so frequently pointed out to me—it would help, it would do me a great deal of good, if I could imagine doing it. So each time I come to you, I want you, once Ginevra has undressed and gone to bed, to put on her clothing, her jewels, and so on. Fix yourself up just like her. Do your hair the way she does. Look as much like her as you can. Then let down the rope ladder. I will come to you pretending that you are she. I have to fool myself like this, Dalinda. It's my only hope, the only way I can get over this.' That's what he said.

"I was beside myself on account of him. I was in no state to realize that what he insisted upon was a fraud, that is, a fraud meant to fool not only himself. It was obvious, but I wasn't myself. And in Ginevra's clothes, I let down the ladder he'd climbed so often already. I didn't see the trap until it was sprung.

"Meanwhile, the duke, who had been Ariodante's friend before their rivalry over Ginevra, said something to him on the lines of 'I can't help wondering why you treat me so badly, when I always respected and loved you as my equal. I know very well that you know about the long-standing love between Ginevra and me. Why do you keep bothering us? Why do you keep your heart set on her, when you know she won't have you? When I am about to ask her father for her hand? I would certainly have some consideration for you, by God, if I were in your place and you were in mine.'

"'And I,' Ariodante answered, 'wonder at you much more. I was in love with her first, and I know that you realize how much Ginevra and I love each other. Nobody could be so much in love. She is longing to be my wife. She doesn't love you, and you know it, and I know you do. I really would respect your feelings, as an old friend, if you were in my position. It's true that you're richer than I am. But that doesn't bother her, or the king, either. I am going to ask, and he will give me her hand, because it's me she wants to marry.'

" 'You've made a great mistake,' said the duke, 'on account of your foolish, hopeless love for her. You believe you are more loved by her; I believe this, too; but one must judge these things by their fruits. Suppose you tell me what proof you think you have from her, and I tell you my own secret. Whoever has less can give up and get himself another love. Of course, I am ready to swear never to repeat anything you tell me; and I would want you to assure me that you won't repeat what I tell you, either.'

"So they agreed, and swore with their hands on the Gospels, and when they had sworn, Ariodante spoke first.

"He told the duke in some detail how it was between Ginevra and himself, how she had sworn to him, to his face and in writing, that she would never marry anyone else. If their marriage were opposed by the king, she had promised him to refuse any other marriage, ever, and to live alone for the rest of her life. He told how he hoped, by the strength of his arm, to earn the praise and honor of the king and the kingdom, and to grow in his lord's grace enough to be considered worthy of having her. Then he said, 'That's the way it is. Those are the terms I'm on with her. Nor do I believe that anyone else comes near, nor do I seek more proof of her love for me. How could I? God reserves the rest for marriage. It would be pointless to ask for more, because she's so good.'

"When Ariodante had told the truth about what he had and what he hoped for, Polinesso, whose aim was to make Ginevra her true lover's enemy, bragged, 'You are nowhere near me. You have said it yourself. You'll have to admit that I'm the one who has hope—and more than hope—when I've told you how I already have—happiness. She is pretending, with you. She doesn't love you. You're nothing to her. You feed on hope and words. When she's with me, she always says your love for her is childish nonsense. As for me, I have more proof of her love than silly promises. I ought to keep quiet about it, but under the terms of our oath, I'll tell you everything.

" 'Not a month passes that I'm not with her three, four, five, sometimes ten nights, in her arms, naked, and sharing our pleasure. You can't compare your idle talk with that. You can't compete with me. Give up and look for somebody else.'

" 'I don't believe you,' protested Ariodante. 'I know you're lying. You've made this thing up to discourage me. But your lie is too much of an insult to her. You will have to support your story, and I will prove that you are not only a liar, but also a traitor, right now.'

" 'It wouldn't be proper to fight over it,' the duke replied, 'since I offer to prove what I say. Whenever you want, I'll let you see, with your own eyes.'

"This did scare Ariodante, and he shuddered. Had he really believed the lie, he would have died right then and there. Transfixed, with pale face, and trembling, bitter voice, he said, 'Whenever you can let me see your rare adventure, I promise to forget her, so liberal to you, so unkind to me. But do not imagine that I will believe you if I do not see it.'

" 'The next time,' Polinesso suggested, 'I will let you know,' and he left.

"I don't think that more than two nights were to pass before the duke was to come to me; bent on springing the trap he had so carefully set, he told his rival that he ought to hide himself that night in the abandoned buildings across from the balcony, and showed him exactly where.

"Ariodante became suspicious that Polinesso's real object in getting him to come there at night was to murder him. Of course, that was not far from the truth. He refused to believe the lie about Ginevra, or Polinesso's boast that he would give visible evidence of her impossible misconduct. He decided to go there nonetheless, but with some protection from ambush so that, if attacked, he could defend himself. He had a wise and daring brother, the most famous fighter at court, Lurcanio; with him, Ariodante felt more confidence than with ten others.

"He called his brother and told him to arm himself, and at night he led him to the place, not that he told him or anyone else what it was all about. Placing Lurcanio a stone's throw away from him, he said, 'If you hear me call, come. But if you don't hear me, don't leave this spot, brother, if you love me.'

" 'Go ahead, and don't worry,' his brother told him.

"So Ariodante went and hid himself in the abandoned building opposite my secret balcony.

"The wicked duke, so eager to defame Ginevra, came by another way and gave the signal we used. And I, knowing nothing of his deceit, in a dress of Ginevra's, white, striped and edged with gold, and with a gold hairnet under a velvet cap decorated with pretty scarlet tassels (a fashion worn only by Ginevra, not by anyone else), went out at his signal onto the balcony, which was built in such a way that I was exposed in front and on either side, as on a stage.

"Lurcanio, meanwhile, afraid that his brother might be in danger, or simply prompted by the common desire to spy on others, had followed very quietly, keeping to the darkest shadows, and was now standing less than ten steps away from him in the same ruin.

"I, ignorant of this, appeared on the balcony in the dress I've described, with, as far as I was concerned, as good effect as ever. The dress could be seen clearly in the moonlight. My being not unlike Ginevra in look and bearing made my face seem to be hers. There was a considerable distance between me and that empty house where the two brothers stood, in the chill and the dark. How natural for them to be deceived.

"Imagine what horror and disgust this roused in Ariodante! What pain and grief! Catching the rope, Polinesso came climbing up to the open gallery. As soon as he arrived, I threw my arms around his neck, not dreaming we were watched. I kissed him on his lips, all over his face, just as usual. And he began to— caress me, with more than usual ardor, to emphasize his fraud. The boy he had led to this foul spectacle stood there desolate, and saw it all. He fell into such despair that he decided to kill himself on the spot, and set the hilt of his sword on the ground so he could wound himself with the point.

"Lurcanio, who had seen the duke mount up to me with great surprise, but did not know who he was, marked his brother's behavior and, hurrying to him, caught him in his arms and prevented him from killing himself in his fury. Had he been a little farther away, had he reached him a moment later, it would have been too late.

" 'Oh, poor, crazy brother!' he cried, 'have you lost your mind? Why let a woman send you to your death? Let all of them go, like clouds in the wind. Or try to kill her. She deserves to die. But save yourself for an honorable death. You don't deserve this. You loved her when you did not know she was cheating you. Since you've seen with your own eyes what kind of woman she is, what a whore she is, it's better to hate her than to hurt yourself. Why not keep that sword you turn against yourself to prove her sin before the king? Let everyone know what she is!'

"Restrained thus by his brother, Ariodante gave up this immediate attempt against his own life, but it did not weaken his set resolve to die. His heart was not merely stung, but broken. He was in agony. He pretended to his brother that his fury had passed, but the next morning, without saying a word to him or anyone else, he set out, led by his mortal desperation. Nor did anyone hear more of him for days and days. Except for his brother and the duke, no one knew what could have made him go away. Everybody was talking about it, in the palace, in the city, in the whole kingdom.

"Then, after eight days, a traveler came before Ginevra at court with the terrible news: Ariodante had drowned in the sea, dead of his own free will, not by any storm raised by the winds; he had dived from a high rock that jutted out over the water.

" 'Before he did it,' the man related, 'he said to me, happening to meet me on the road, "Come with me so you can tell Ginevra what becomes of me; and then tell her that the reason for what you're about to see is that I have seen too much. That's all. I've seen too much. I wish I had been born blind." We happened to be on Capobasso,' the man went on, 'far out, and so high, pointing toward Ireland. And when he had said what I told you, he jumped, head first, over the edge, and I saw him hit the water and go under. I left and hurried here, a long, long trip for me, to bring you the news.'

"Ginevra was left half dead by this announcement. Oh, God, what she said and did when she found herself alone again in her own dear bed! How she beat her breast and tore her gown and even her golden hair! And in wonder she kept repeating the words that Ariodante had said at the end: 'I've seen too much . . . I've seen too much.'

"The news that he had killed himself spread everywhere. You couldn't find a dry eye at court. His brother showed the most grief, of course; and he drowned himself so deep in sorrow that he almost followed his brother's example, almost turned his hand against himself, to follow him. And, telling himself again and again that it was Ginevra who killed his brother, and that nothing had driven him to his death but her sinister betrayal, he blinded himself with his wish for revenge. He let his rage and grief so overcome him that he did not care at all if he lost the good graces of the king and all the country and earned their hatred.

"Going before the king when the hall was full of people, she said, 'Know, lord, that your daughter alone is guilty of driving my brother out of his mind, so that he went to his death; for his soul was so stricken with pain by having seen how impure and unchaste she is, that death was the only thing he wanted.

" 'He was her suitor, and his intentions were honorable, and I will not keep this quiet: through faithful service and virtue he hoped he would deserve to be given her for his wife. But while he stood aside, and merely inhaled the fragrance of the foliage, he saw another climb, clamber up the forbidden tree and take all the fruit he wanted.' And he went on to tell how he had seen Ginevra come to the balcony, let down the ladder, and greet her paramour. But he could not say who the man was, because he was so muffled up that he could not see his face or even his hair. And he added that he was willing to prove what he said with his sword.

"You can imagine how her father felt about the charge. He never would have thought it of his daughter. He also knew that it would be necessary, if no warrior chose to take up her defense, to condemn her to death. I gather, my lord, that our law is not new to you: any

woman proved to have had sexual intercourse with anyone except her husband goes to her death in one month,
if no knight is strong enough to oppose her accuser and
prove she is innocent.

"In an attempt to save her, the king has proclaimed
that he will give her hand in marriage, with a great
dowry, to any knight who will clear her. But no one has
spoken up for her. On the contrary, they all eye each
other, and wait, because Lurcanio is so fierce that
they're all afraid of him. Perverse Fortune has also
willed that Zerbino, her brother, is not to be found in
the kingdom. Many months ago, he went away, to
prove himself in arms. If he were near enough to get
the news in time, he would not fail to help his sister,
but he has not been found.

"Meanwhile, the king tried to find some other way,
besides the trial by combat, to find out if the charge
is true or false. He apprehended certain maids and
ladies-in-waiting who ought to know, he thought. I
heard about it and realized that if I were taken, it would
be more than dangerous for the duke and me, so that
same night I escaped from the palace and went to the
duke, to warn him about it. If I were caught, I pointed
out, both our heads might fall. He thanked me and told
me not to be afraid, and persuaded me to go to a
fortress of his that is near this place, with two men he
gave me for guides.

"You have heard, my lord, how much and how often
I proved to Polinesso that I loved him. You may decide
for yourself how much he owed me. Now you see the
reward he thinks I deserve. Tell me if any woman ought
to hope she is loved, however much she loves. For that
ungrateful, perfidious, unnaturally cruel fiend doubted
me, at the end, had come to suspect that sometime I
might expose his clever fraud. He pretended that he
wanted to send me to his fortress in the wilderness,

until the king's fury and anger cooled. And all he really wanted was to send me straight to my death. Secretly, he had given orders to those men to take me into the woods and pay back my fidelity with death. And his orders would have been carried out, if you had not been near enough to hear me scream. See how well Love treats his followers!"

Hearing all this from Dalinda as he rode on his way, the knight considered it very lucky to have found the girl who could tell him the whole story of fair Ginevra's innocence. He had hoped to help her even if she were justly accused; now that he knew the charge was false, he was even surer that he would succeed if he arrived in time.

And he rode as fast as Baiardo could run toward the city of Saint Andrews, where the case had to be tried by single combat before the king and all his court.

Near the city, only a few miles distant, they met a squire who had fresher news: a strange knight had come and had undertaken to defend Ginevra. This knight had an unknown coat of arms and kept his face hidden, so that no one had ever seen it. And his own squire who served him vowed, "I do not know who he is."

Soon they were at the walls, and at the gate itself. Dalinda was afraid to go inside, but Rinaldo comforted her and promised her his protection.

The gate, however, was shut.

Asking the keeper, "What does this mean?" Rinaldo was told that all the people were gone to see the fight between Lurcanio and an unknown knight on the far side of the walled town, where there was a broad, flat meadow. As far as the gatekeeper knew, the fight had already begun. He opened the gate to the lord of Montalbano, and quickly shut it again behind him. Rinaldo passed through the empty city, pausing only to leave the girl at the first inn. He told her to stay there, where he was sure she would be safe until he returned to her, which he promised would be soon. Then he hurried on, to the other wall, the other gate, open to the field where the two warriors had begun their deadly give-and-take; the trial was going on. Lurcanio's hatred of Ginevra had not cooled and he fought well; while the anonymous knight defending her well upheld the favorite side.

There were six knights in armor on foot with them inside the fence, and with them was the Duke of Albany, mounted on a powerful courser of noble breed. As lord constable, he had charge of the field and the great crowd around it; and he watched the fight with pleasure and pride.

Rinaldo made his way through the throng. Everyone made way for Baiardo; no one who heard the storm of his hoofbeats was too lame or lazy to get out of the way in time. Polinesso of Albany scarcely had time to realize a knight was riding through the mob before Rinaldo, appearing preeminent, the flower of all knighthood, was already facing the king where he sat watching the sad trial; and everyone crowded so close to hear what he had to say, filling the space behind and all around him, that no one hindered him.

And Rinaldo said to the king, "Great lord, do not let the combat continue. Whichever of these two men dies, know that you would let him die unjustly. The one thinks that he is in the right, and is mistaken, and speaks falsely but does not know that he lies; but the same error that killed his brother has put that sword in his hand.

"The other does not know if he is right or wrong, but only through chivalry and goodness has put himself in mortal peril, not to let such beauty die.

"I bring salvation for the innocent; I bring damnation to him who lies.

"But first, for God's sake, stop this fight! Then listen to what I have to tell you."

The king was so moved by the authority of Rinaldo's aspect and bearing that he gave the word and made the sign that the fight was over. Then Rinaldo told him, his knights and his people about the plot Polinesso had laid for Ginevra. Afterwards, he promised to prove by arms that what he said was true. Polinesso was called, and he stepped forward, looking troubled; but he boldly began to deny his guilt.

Rinaldo interrupted him, saying, "Let's prove it, now."

And as both were armed, and the field was ready, they began without delay.

The king and the people hoped that Ginevra would be proven innocent, as they had hoped during the long, inconclusive combat before. Everyone hoped that God would show clearly that she had unjustly been called lewd. And few would object to its being proved on Polinesso, rather than on Lurcanio, who made the charge, because the Duke of Albany had a reputation for pride, greed and falsehood. No one had been surprised by Rinaldo's account of his plot.

Another noble now took charge of the lists, and Polinesso, obviously frightened, put his lance in the rest at the sound of the third trumpet. Rinaldo did the same, hoping to finish him in a blow, and aiming for his chest. They rode against each other, and Rinaldo had his wish; the point of his lance caught Polinesso, piercing his armor, his ribs and his back. At least half the lance was driven through his body until it caught where the shaft widened, and he was carried to the ground more than six yards away from his fine destrier.

Rinaldo dismounted quickly, grabbed Polinesso's

helmet and unlaced it before he could move, even had he been able to. Then he realized that Polinesso could make no more war. Polinesso humbly begged him for mercy, though he could have no more use for it.

"Confess," said Rinaldo.

With an effort at words, faint yet audible to the king and the court, Polinesso confessed the fraud that had destroyed him. He did not finish it all; in the middle of the story, voice and life both left him.

The king, seeing his daughter freed from shame and death, was happier than if, having lost his crown, he had that moment recovered it, and he did Rinaldo high honor. When the knight took off his helmet, the king recognized him, having met him before. He raised his hands to God, who had provided the deliverer.

That other knight, still unknown, who had helped Ginevra before Rinaldo's arrival, was standing apart, listening to everything, but saying nothing. The king begged him to tell his name, too, or at least show his face, so that he might be properly rewarded. Finally, he unlaced his helmet, lifted it, and let them see what I have to put in the next chapter—if you would like to hear the rest of the story.

SIX

The Enchantment of Astolfo

Woe to the evildoer who trusts that his crime will stay
hidden forever! For when all else is still, the air and the
very earth in which it is buried may reveal it; and God
often lets the sin drive the sinner to give himself away,
even after he has gotten away with it and no one questions him. Miserable Polinesso had intended to cover
his crime completely by disposing of Dalinda, the only
person who knew about it besides himself; and in adding this second crime to the first, brought on himself the
unhappy end that he had hoped to put off, losing
friends, rank and life at one and the same time, and, a
much more serious loss, all honor, too.

I told you how everyone begged the unknown knight
to show himself, and how at last he took off his helmet.
He uncovered a face all of them knew and loved: he was
Ariodante, who had been mourned throughout Scotland, Ariodante, for whom Ginevra, the king, the court
and all the people had mourned because he was so good
and brave.

It transpired that the traveler had lied in reporting
his death, although it was quite true that the man had
seen Ariodante dive off the cliff into the sea. But it
often happens that desperate people who long for death
when it is not near at hand, hate it when they see it
come close, the step from misery to death still being a
serious one. So Ariodante changed his mind about dying
when he found himself deep in the cold, green water.

And because he was as strong and quick and brave as the next man, he came up for air, started to swim and made it back to shore. Realizing that suicide is senseless, he climbed the rocks and, soaking wet, eventually came to a hermit's cell on the coast.

He decided to wait there in secret until he had heard the news of his own death and then heard whether Ginevra was happy about it, or moved to pity. In time, because everybody was talking about it, he heard that she was almost dead from grief herself. This was not what he would have expected, after he had seen how she welcomed Polinesso. Then he heard that his brother Lurcanio had accused Ginevra of that crime before the king. This angered him, and he realized he still loved her. Even if he had not, his brother's charge would have seemed unjust and cruel to him, though he knew it was brought on his behalf, or maybe because he knew it. He also heard that no knight was willing to appear in her defense, on account of Lurcanio's well-deserved reputation for strength, skill and bravery. Besides, those who knew him personally were sure that he was careful, wise and discreet, and would not bring false charges against anyone. If the charge were true, how could anyone be expected to defend her, anyway? No one cares to defend the wrong, when the end is death.

Ariodante considered all this, and decided at last to oppose his brother's accusation.

"Alas," he said to himself, "I cannot bear to think of her dying on account of me; my own death would be too bitter if I saw her die before me like that. She is still my lady and my goddess, the only light of my eyes; right or wrong, I must try to rescue her and fall dead on the field. I know this means supporting the wrong and I will die for it. So be it. And I know that after my death the beautiful girl still has to die. My only comfort in dying will be that even if her Polinesso does love her, she will be able to see clearly how little, since he doesn't trouble himself to help her, while I die. In spite of her betrayal of me, she'll see me die trying to save her. I'll show my brother, too. He'll see where this kind of cruelty leads. He'll think he's avenging me, and then he will learn that he has killed me with his own hand."

Having made up his mind, he got new arms and a new horse, and he wore a black surcoat and carried a black shield edged with apple-green. He managed to find a squire unknown in that part of the country to follow him, and, unknown himself, as I've told you, he presented himself armed against his brother. And I've told you how it turned out, and how he was recognized.

The king was as happy to see him as he had been when his daughter was freed, a moment before. And he thought to himself that a truer and more faithful lover never could be found, one who, after such a betrayal, imaginary though it was, took up her defense against his own brother, though he believed it was hopeless. Following his own inclination (for he loved him very much) and the petitions of his whole court, and of Rinaldo who insisted most of all, he made Ariodante his fair daughter's consort. The duchy of Albany, which reverted to the king on Polinesso's death, could not have fallen vacant at a better time; the king made it his daughter's dowry.

Rinaldo begged mercy for Dalinda, and she went free. Tired of the world, she turned her mind to God and vowed to become a nun in Denmark, and she left Scotland at once.

But by now it's time to return to Ruggiero, crossing the sky on the swift hippogriff.

He kept his spirits up; he did not grow pale or faint; but his heart trembled in his breast like a leaf in the wind. He had left all Europe far behind; he was far beyond the sign that the invincible Hercules had set up to warn sailors—those pillars at the entrance to the Atlantic Ocean. The great, strange bird-beast, the hippogriff, bore him on his way with such speed that they would have left Jupiter's thunderbolts far behind. No other flying thing could match his velocity. The roar and flash of the thunderbolt cannot come down from Heaven to Earth more quickly than he flew.

After the creature had traversed a great space in a straight line without rest, he tired of the air at last, and began to circle, swoop and descend over an island even fairer then Ortygia, where the virgin nereid Arethusa fled in vain from her lover, the god of the sacred river Alpheus. (She fled under the bottom of the sea—a journey as strange as Ruggiero's—but her lover followed her and took her on Ortygia.)

This was an island that could not have been fairer. Search all the world by air, and you will not find one so beautiful and pleasant. And as the hippogriff descended, circling, Ruggiero could see all its beauty increasing in detail—the cultivated plains and smooth hills, the clear waters, the shady shorelines and lush, well-watered meadows. There were mountains, and he thought he saw a thread of gold along the base of one of them, but that was to one side, and soon out of sight. Below him, there were groves of sweet laurel, of palm and of myrtle, of cedar and of orange bearing fruit and flower—all composed in varied forms, all beautiful and all offering ample refuge from the torrid heat of summer days in that climate. Among their branches, the nightingale safely flew singing. Ruggiero could hear, then see them. And by that time he could see the crimson roses and white lilies, always kept fresh by temperate breezes, and hares and rabbits and stags with their proud, high horns, all grazing on the green lawns without fear that anyone would hunt and kill them. Some stood still, and watched, but none of them tried to flee from the hippogriff's sailing shadow.

As soon as the hippogriff was so close to the ground that the fall could not be dangerous, Ruggiero hastily slid out of the saddle and sprawled on the enameled green. He did not let go of the reins, though. He did not want to lose his mount, which landed beside him. He tied it to a green myrtle, between a bay and a pine, near the margin of the sea.

Nearby, there was a spring, surrounded by lemon trees and palms; he put his own shield off his tired arm, lifted the heavy helmet from his sweating brow, and pulled off his gauntlets. He turned his face to the fresh, life-giving breezes that stirred and rustled all that well-kept, parklike wood, now from the quiet sea and now from the snow-capped mountain visible from this spot on the shore. He wet his dried lips again and again in the clear, fresh water from the spring, and he splashed his hands in the little pond in order to cool his face and his whole body. He was very hot, from the sun and the wind. He had traveled, without landing, without pause, fully armed, long and far into the sinking sun—and here, somewhere in the Indies, it was still sinking.

While he drank, washed and rested, the steed he had tied in the cool shade of the thickest foliage took fright at something and made the myrtle he was tied to shake so much that a shower of leaves fell on and all around him. Not able to get loose, he gave up. But the tree went on trembling, much more than it would from the gentle breeze that was blowing, and leaves still fell on the hippogriff. Ruggiero got up and went to the tree.

Like a burning log, with pockets filled with air and moisture, hissing and boiling until the wood explodes, so the tree, still shuddering, made strange, muffled sounds until at last its bark burst open, like a mouth, with a shriek. And then a voice spoke from the tree, sadly and feebly, but with very clear enunciation, saying, "If you are as courteous as your appearance suggests, please untie this animal. Isn't my punishment for sin and folly bad enough, without being tortured from outside my bark?"

When Ruggiero was sure the voice did indeed come from the tree, he was astonished. He quickly untied the hippogriff and stood there, holding the reins, blushing and saying, "Pardon me, whatever you may be, whether a human spirit or a goddess of the wood. I've disturbed your beautiful—boughs. But I didn't know that some spirit was hiding underneath your bark. Nevertheless, now that I know there is a rational spirit in this shape, please tell me who or what you are. And may Heaven always shield you from hail. And if I am ever able to make up for this damage, with some good deed, I swear by my fair lady that I shall speak or act or do both in such a way as to earn your thanks in the future, if . . ."

As Ruggiero ended his speech, the tree trembled from crown to roots once again. Then he saw that it was sweating through its rough bark, like fresh wood near the fire. It began to speak again.

"Your courtesy," it said, "obliges me to explain to you at once who I was before, and who turned me into this myrtle tree on this pleasant seashore.

"My name was Astolfo, and I was a paladin and peer of France, dreaded in war—enough. I was cousin to Orlando and Rinaldo, whose fame is boundless. I see you have heard of them, too. I was heir to the whole kingdom of England, after my father Ottone, the present king. And I was so charming and comely that I made more than one lady love me dearly—and at last hurt only myself.

"Coming home, after the siege of Albracca, from that ultimate island of the East Indies, Demongir, where Rinaldo and I and some others had been imprisoned in a dark pit until we were freed by the supreme force of Orlando, the knight of Brava, we were going westward over the sands of a shore where the North wind raged furiously. And the shore, and my evil destiny, brought us one morning to a fine beach where one of the castles belonging to the powerful Alcina stands by the sea. We found Alcina at home. Rather, she had come out to stand alone at the edge of the deep, where without net or hook she was drawing all the fish she wanted to the shore. We wondered, as we came around the last rocky headland before we got to her castle, because out at sea there was white water, from all the fish jumping, and we could hear a sound that was not quite like the waves.

"And there she stood, the fish rushing toward her— the dolphins, the fat tunnies with their mouths open, the sperm whales and the seals and sea cows, roused from their lazy rest and panting. Mullets, sailfish, salpouth, salmon and raven fish swimming in schools all marshaling as quickly as they could. The monstrous backs of sawfish, sperm whales, orcs and sharks burst from the boiling froth. Eels wriggled up out of the water at her feet. Other things leaped, flopped or crawled. Schools and herds of sea creatures, great and small, and those huge, solitary monsters.

"Among them we saw a whale that was the biggest ever seen in any ocean, I'm sure. I can't tell you how many paces wide his shoulders were, above the salt waves. We all thought, because he was steady and never moved, that he was a rather small island. It was wide, and it was also so high that you couldn't see the farther shore.

"Alcina was calling to all these things, and making

the ones she really wanted come out of the water. She did this simply by chanting magic at them. I don't know what she could have done with them all. She just called them.

"Alcina was born with Morgan le Fay, you know. I can't say if it was one delivery, or if not, which is older, or how many fays there are in that whole family. They used to live together on an island in the North Sea, you know. That was long ago, but they're immortal. Now they occupy islands here and there around the world.

"Anyway, Alcina looked at me, and I could tell that my good looks pleased her right away. You know how it is. I could tell by her reaction. And she decided to take me away from my friends, and she managed to do it. Not that it was difficult for her. She saw us, saw me, stopped chanting. The fish started to sink, swim, scatter, escape. I noticed that, although it was hard to notice anything except the sorceress as she came toward us—that face, smiling, and such a gracious, dignified manner.

"She said, more to me than to the others, 'Knights, if it pleases you to lodge with me today, I will show you my catch—all the fish of all the different kinds there are: scaly, soft and smooth or hairy, all wet and wriggling. Wonderful things come to me, out of the deeps, and more of them than the stars in the sky. Right now, if you would like to see a siren (for they obey me, too), just step this way to the other shore.' And she indicated that monstrous whale.

As I said, we had all assumed that whale was an island. I was always willful. I regret it now. I followed right after her. Rinaldo signaled me, and so did Dudon. I knew they didn't want me to go, but I paid no attention. Fata Alcina urged me on, with her smiling face. It was a bit of a climb up the whale's back, and she was just behind me, saying something about the siren. I can't remember what she said. And I didn't realize until I was on top of the monster that there was just the other side of it, and by then we were moving out to sea.

"The whale did it very well, I must say. It was a very smooth ride, from beginning to end. Anyway, by the time I realized how stupid I had been, we were too far from the shore.

"Rinaldo dived into the water and swam after to save me, and he almost drowned, because a furious south wind rose suddenly, with dark clouds out of nowhere. I know he turned back. I don't know if he made it."

"He did," said Ruggiero. "He's back in France."

"It's a comfort to hear it," said the tree who had been Astolfo. "Alcina comforted me on the back of the whale, of course. All that day and all the next night she had me on top of that monster in the middle of the ocean.

"At last we came to this beautiful island. Alcina holds a great part of it. She usurped it from a sister of hers. Not Morgana, but a legitimate sister. Somebody who knew the whole story told me that Alcina and Morgana were born of incest or some such. They are thoroughly wicked, full of every brutal vice you could imagine, while their legitimate sister lives in chastity and has set all her heart on all the virtues. The two wicked ones conspire against her, and make war. Any number of times Alcina has invaded her good sister's lands, on this island and on others, with her bestial troops, driving her from one place to another. And the good one, who is named Logistilla, wouldn't have a chance of holding any ground here, if it weren't for the bay and the uninhabitable mountains dividing this island, just as Scotland and England have water and mountains between them, separating the two kingdoms on the one island. But of course Alcina and Morgana will not rest until they have taken everything from Logistilla. They are so guilty that they hate her just because she is so pure and holy.

"But to go back to what I was telling you, about how I became a tree. Alcina kept me here. She burned with love for me, and I really loved her, too. She was so beautiful, so sweet. I took great pleasure in her delicate —very delicate—flesh. When I had her, it seemed to me that I'd harvested all the good that is divided up among us mortals all over the world. One gets more, another gets less, and nobody gets very much; but I thought I had it all. I didn't remember France, or anything or anyone else. I didn't do a thing but love her, I didn't think of anything else; every thought ended in her.

"And she loved me just as much as I loved her. She didn't care for any of the others any more. She had left all her other lovers—for there certainly were others before me. And I advised her about everything. She had me at her side day and night. I gave orders for her. She seemed to delight in taking orders from me. She didn't even talk to anyone else.

"Oh, why must I touch my old wounds? I have no hope that they'll ever heal. Why must I remember the good that I had, when I suffer such punishment for it now? Just when I believed myself to be happy, when I believed Alcina must love me forever, she took back her heart and gave it to another. I realized too late how fickle she was. I didn't reign here as her consort for more than two months before a new lover took my place. I fell from her good graces, and she drove me away with scorn, and then I learned that she had treated a thousand others to a similar end, all most unfairly, as in my case.

"And to prevent them from going all over the world

(for that's where they come from, of course), telling tales about her lasciviousness, she plants them here and there throughout this pleasant land, changing them into firs, olive trees, palms, fruit trees, or myrtles, as you see. She turns others into beasts, and some she just melts into water, they say, to make fountains and pools, I suppose. In short, into whatever most pleases that proud fay at the moment.

"Now you, my lord, have come to this fatal island in an unusual manner. Whether you came on your own, or she brought you here on that thing, makes no difference. Some lover of hers (I wonder how many, since me) will be turned to stone or water or something as soon as she sees you. And you will hold scepter and lordship from Alcina, and you will be happy above all other mortals; but you will surely come to the same pass soon—wood, water, stone, or beast.

"I have willingly given you fair warning. Not that I believe it will do you any good. But it may be better for you if you don't go into it blindly. Perhaps, as your face is different, your talents and intelligence may be different, too. Perhaps you will know how to avoid the harm that has befallen a thousand others before you."

Ruggiero, who had known that his lady Bradamante had an English cousin named Astolfo, was very sorry that he had been turned from his true form into a useless and miserable tree; and for love of that lady he would have served her cousin, if he had known how; but he could not help in any other way but by comforting him. He did this as best he could, assuring the tree-knight that the damage might be undone. Then he asked if there were a way that led to the realm of the good Logistilla, either over the plain or hills, so that he need not stay in Alcina's lands.

There was no other way, the tree told him, save

over the mountains, through very high, wild, rocky land. But, the tree added, he could not expect to get as far as the mountains without meeting a horde of fierce creatures who would drive him back. Alcina kept them all along the border so that no one could get away.

Ruggiero thanked the myrtle for everything, and left forewarned. He pulled his flying steed after him, and it followed willingly enough on its claws and hoofs. He did not mount it, because he had no idea where it might take him next—maybe to Alcina herself. He thought that he would make it on foot over the mountains, into Logistilla's country, and save himself. He had firmly decided to use every means possible to avoid Alcina and prevent her from getting any power over him.

I'm strong enough to cross over, if I don't lose the way, he said to himself. But in vain.

He was not two miles along the seashore, toward the blue, white-capped mountains, when he saw the beautiful city of Alcina, or rather its awesome wall, which seemed to lie under the mountain and by the sea. He saw it from far away. It was very long and high and where the mountains did not rise behind it, the wall itself seemed to touch the sky. It appeared to be of gold from top to bottom.

(Someone may dispute me on this point and say that it was just alchemy, and maybe he's wrong, and then again he might know more about such things than I do. But it looked like gold because it shone like gold.)

There was a good road leading to the jeweled gate, but Ruggiero crossed it, turning to the right and walking over open meadows that rose to the mountains. But soon he met with the evil band lying in the long grass; they stood up and tried to stop him, as Astolfo had warned.

There never was seen a stranger, more monstrous and ill-formed mob. The faces were especially grotesque. Some had human shapes from the neck down, but had heads like monkeys or cats. Some stamped the grass with goats' feet. Others were centaurs. Some of them were naked, while others were wrapped in weird skins and furs. All who were human enough to show their age looked like shameless youths or silly old fools. Some rode without reins on horses. Others rode slowly on asses or oxen or the centaurs, or even on ostriches and giant cranes. Some put horns to their mouths and sounded them, and others drank from them. Some were female, some male, others both. They were carrying strange weapons: a hook, a rope ladder, an iron shovel, or the sort of silent file thieves use.

The captain of this band had a swollen belly and a puffy, greasy face. He came slumped on a giant tortoise that lurched forward very slowly. He had creatures on either side to support him, because he was drunk and almost unconscious; some others wiped his brow and his drooling chin; and still others fanned him.

The first to come near Ruggiero, one who had a human body but the neck and head of a dog, howled at him that he must go into the fair city that stood behind him.

The knight answered, "I will not go there while I have enough strength left in my hand to hold this," and he drew his sword and pointed it at the dog-headed man.

The monster would have wounded him with a spear, but Ruggiero quickly rushed at him and gave him a thrust in the belly that emerged a hand's breadth from the back. At the same time, he put his shield on his arm and, without a pause, ran into the mob to clear his way. But his enemies came before him in too great a number; here one stung him, there another clutched him, while he defended himself and made hard war against them. He could strike them down easily enough, splitting them to the teeth, to the chest, and lopping off their arms, for they had no helmets, cuirasses, or any other armor, and they carried no shields. But they came at him from all sides, so that he would have had to be equipped with a hundred arms, or maybe more, to advance through the vile race.

If he had thought of uncovering the magic shield that the wizard Atlante had left tied to the hippogriff's saddle, he would have conquered the brutal mob immediately, making all of them fall blind and unconscious around him. But maybe he did not think of that in time, or maybe he scorned an easy, magical victory, because he would rather rely on his own strength and skill than on fraud. Be that as it may, he would rather die than surrender to such low things, and so the fight went on inconclusively.

But meanwhile, behold, from the gate in the golden wall two young ladies came riding on a unicorn. By their manner and dress, they apparently were not born humbly nor brought up by shepherds, in hardship, but nobly and among the pleasures of some royal palace. Their unicorn was whiter than the whitest ermine. Both were beautiful and of such elaborate dress, with an air so refined, that a man would have to have divine eyesight to judge between them; Beauty and Grace, if they had flesh, would look like those ladies.

They rode up behind Ruggiero, now sorely pressed by the villainous rabble, and all his enemies got out of their way. The ladies came to Ruggiero and extended their hands to him. He blushed and thanked them for their kindness, and was happy to please them by going back to that golden gate he had fought so hard to escape.

The ornamentation that turned and twisted over the

gate, jutting out beyond it, high above, had no segment that was not encrusted with the rarest gems of the East. At four corners this canopy of jewels was supported by gross columns of monolithic crystal. Whether what one saw here was true or false, it was most impressive. On the threshold and around the columns, girls ran and sported. Had they retained a little dignity, they might have looked even fairer. They were all dressed in green gowns, and crowned with fresh, green leaves. They made Ruggiero, still on foot, with the hippogriff in tow, feel more than welcome by their behavior, as he passed through the open gate into their paradise. You could call it Paradise, truly enough, if the place itself were true; you would believe that Love himself was born there. No one could stay there except in dancing and sporting. Everyone had to spend all his hours in festival. Aged thoughts and cares were not permitted to lodge in any heart; care and want were banished, and Plenty was always there with her horn overflowing. April, with serene and joyous look, seemed to smile forever there on all the youths and maidens. Near a fountain, one was singing in a sweet, enchanting voice; in the shade of a tree, another sported or danced or did something pleasurable; and still another, far away from the others, practiced his complaints of love on one faithful friend. Through the crowns of pine and laurel, of beech and shaggy fir, sporting infant Loves were flying. Some rejoiced happily over victories, while others took aim to shoot lovers' hearts, or spread nets to trap them. One was tempering arrows in a brook, and another sharpened them on a grindstone.

Then a great courser was given to Ruggiero. It was strong and big and light reddish-brown, and it had beautiful trimmings embroidered with precious stones and fine gold thread. His winged courser, which used to obey the ancient Moor, was left to a youth who led it after the good Ruggiero at a less hurried pace.

Those two beautiful and amorous ladies who had protected Ruggiero from the mob in the meadow under the mountain, now turned to him and, speaking for both, one of them said to him, "Sir, your virtuous works, which we have just seen, seem so daring to us, that we will boldly ask your help on our behalf. We will soon come to a marsh that divides this garden in two parts. A cruel creature who calls herself Erifilia keeps the bridge, and seizes and robs anybody who wants to go from one side to the other. She is gigantic, with long teeth and a poisonous bite, and sharp nails like a bear. Besides always blocking our way, which would be free if not for her, she often runs wild all through the garden, disturbing this and that. And you ought to know about the murderous folk who attacked you outside the gate; many of them are her sons, and all are her followers—impudent, impious, inhospitable and rapacious, like her."

"For you," Ruggiero responded, "I am ready to fight not only one battle, but a hundred. With my person, for what it's worth, you may do as you please, because the reason I wear plate and mail is not to earn land or silver, but only to do good to others—especially to beautiful ladies like you."

The ladies thanked him profusely, as befitted such a knight, and as they chatted thus, they came over a graceful little hill and saw the bridge and the shore. They also saw the proud giantess Erifilla, ornamented with emerald and sapphire on her golden armor.

But I postpone telling how Ruggiero put himself in danger with her; it's too late to go into that in this chapter.

SEVEN

The Island of Alcina

A man who travels far from this own country sees things very different from what he might have expected, but when he tells people about them afterwards, he is not believed and is called a liar. The common fools who stay at home are not willing to believe in anything they cannot see and touch, clearly and plainly. For this reason, I know that inexperienced readers will not wholly believe my story. Whether they believe a lot or little, I don't have to pay attention to the ignorant rabble. I know very well that you will believe me, because you obviously have the light of reason, and can think for yourself. I am working to please you; I don't care about them.

I left off as they came to the bank and the bridge that avaricious Erifilla was guarding.

She wore the finest metal armor, adorned with gems of many colors, with red rubies, yellow chrysolites, green emeralds, tawny jacinths, and so on. Over the armor, the damned pest had a sand-colored surcoat. Except for the color, it was the kind that bishops and cardinals wear at court. And on her shield and crest she had the sign of a swollen and venomous toad. She was mounted, but not on a horse; instead, she surged forward, over the bridge, on a giant wolf equipped with a preposterously rich saddle. I do not believe that there are wolves that big even in Apulia; it was as big as an ox. I do not know how she managed to make it go as she wished; there was no bit in its frothing jaws.

The ladies did not have to point her out to Ruggiero, nor explain how she made the public bridge her tilting field; she was riding toward him, to disgrace him and block his way, as she so often did to others. She roared at Ruggiero, telling him to turn back. Taking a lance, he defied her challenge. She was no less ardent, and spurred the monstrous wolf, setting herself in the jeweled saddle and putting her lance in the rest. The whole bridge swayed and trembled as the wolf raced across.

Still, she was left on the meadow at the fierce encounter, for the good Ruggiero caught her under the helmet and drove her out of the saddle with such force that she was thrown backward over six yards. He drew his sword and went to cut off her huge head. It would not have been any trouble, because she was lying like a corpse on the flowers and the grass. But the ladies shouted, "It's enough that she's beaten, without taking more revenge! Sheathe your sword, courteous knight. Let us cross the bridge and go on our way."

On the other side, they had to go up a rather rough road. Besides being narrow and stony, it went almost straight up the hillside. But when they reached the top, they were on a broad meadowland in view of the most fair and pleasant palace that anyone could ever see in this world.

And the beautiful Alcina came out of the main gate and part way across the lawn to Ruggiero, receiving him in her noble way in the midst of her lovely and adoring court. And all those fair folk of hers did such reverence to the strong young warrior that they could not have done more if God had descended among them from Heaven. Alcina's palace was excellent not only in its wealth, but even more in its courtly creatures.

They differed from each other very little in their blooming youth and beauty; but Alcina was by far the most
beautiful of all, as the sun is more beautiful than all
the stars.

Alcina's entire face and figure appeared to be as
well formed as an industrious artist's rendering of the
ideal. Her blonde hair was long and tangled, and like
a gold frame around her face. Gold could not shine
more than did her hair. On her delicate cheeks the
colors of rose and jasmine were perfectly blended. Her
smooth brow was like bright ivory, and perfectly proportioned. Under two black, slender arches were two
dark eyes—rather, two clear black suns, charitable,
even compassionate, in their look, and sober and eco-
nomical in their movement. Around them, Love seemed
to sport, hovering, discharging all the arrows in his
quiver, taking all hearts away. Envy could find nothing
to change about her nose, which was neither too large
nor too small and set precisely in the middle of her
face. Beneath it, as between two dales, was the mouth
spread with native vermilion; the beautiful lips hid and
disclosed two strings of choice pearls, as she made
polite speeches that would render pliant the roughest,
rawest hearts; and her smile seemed to open, at her
pleasure, paradise on Earth. Her neck was like snow;
her breasts, like milk. The neck was round and smooth,
the breasts were full, two tender apples of pure ivory
that rose and fell like waves at the shore when a
pleasant breeze caresses still waters. Argus with his
hundred eyes could not have spied out the rest, but
anyone would judge that what she hid was in accord
with what she exposed. Her arms were evidently im-
maculately proportioned, and her white hand, glimpsed
often below her sleeve, was long and slender, with no
protruding veins. You could catch glimpses of her feet,
too, not long but also slender, and well rounded, to

complement her august figure. She looked, in short, like an angel born in Heaven, and no veil, no matter how voluminous, could obscure the impression; in every feature and in everything she did, she set a noose, a snare, whether she spoke or smiled or moved a step, or simply stood still.

It was no wonder that Ruggiero was taken as soon as he looked and found her so incomparable. What he had heard from the myrtle tree earlier, how treacherous and evil she was, was no help to him now; he did not believe that treason or even trickery could co-exist with so sweet a smile. Instead, he chose to believe that Astolfo had been transmuted on the shore for his own ungrateful behavior, that he must have deserved it, and more besides. He decided that all he had heard about her was false, and that spite, envy, malice or revenge led that wretched tree to blame her and lie about everything.

He suddenly forgot the beautiful girl he had loved so much, so long, for with her magic Alcina drugged all the wounds of former loves, and with her love alone she impressed him, so that in his heart she alone was engraved. So the good Ruggiero ought to be excused if here he showed himself inconstant.

At Alcina's table, zithers, harps, lyres and other assorted instruments made the surrounding air ring with delicious melody and harmony. There also was a singer, with poetic inventions about the joys, the pains and the fulfillment of love. And what triumphant and sumptuous board spread by any successor of Ninus, from Semiramis to Sardanapalus, or that eternally famous and celebrated feast spread by Cleopatra for the Latin conqueror, could equal the one that the loving fay had set before the paladin Ruggiero? I cannot believe that there is feasting like that even where Ganymede serves the sublime Jupiter. When

the viands and the tables were removed, they played
an easy game, sitting in a circle, giving the lovers
an opportunity to whisper in each other's ears whatever they wanted, without inhibition. And they agreed
to meet again together that night.

The game was over soon, much sooner than usual.
Then pages came carrying torches, to chase the gloom
from the palace with bright red light. Surrounded by
the fair company, Ruggiero was brought to a fresh,
decorated chamber chosen for him as the most befitting, with a huge feather bed. After sweetmeats,
wine and politeness, they left him, bowing to him
reverently, and all of them went to their rooms, or
at least, to other rooms. Then Ruggiero undressed
and slid between the perfumed linens, so smooth they
seemed to have come from the hands of Arachne. But
all the time he kept his ears alert against the lovely
lady's coming.

At each hint of sound, he raised his head, hoping
it was she. Often he only thought he heard, but there
was no sound at all. He would hold his breath, waiting,
and sigh after each disappointment. Sometimes he got
out of the bed and opened the door, stared out and
found nothing there; and a thousand times he thoroughly cursed the hour that took so long to pass. Saying
to himself, Now she's starting, she's coming, he would
begin to count the imaginary steps that might lie between her room and his. He would reach some high
figure, and lose the count, fearful of missing her foot-
step. He had more vivid thoughts, too. And often he
became afraid that something had come between his
hands and the fruit, something had happened and she
would not come at all.

Alcina eventually tired of perfuming herself all over,
expensively, and decided that it was time. She sat a
while longer, listening, and hearing no sound anywhere

in her palace, she crept out of her room and came quietly down a secret corridor to the room where Ruggiero's heart struggled with hope and fear.

He did not hear her approach, and did not know how long she stood there; happening to look up, once, his eyes met those smiling stars of hers, hanging over him. If he had suffered before, now he felt sulphur burning in his veins, unable to contain himself, and soon he was swimming, submerged up to the eyes, at least, in the gulf of delightful and beautiful things. He jumped out of bed and took her in his arms, and could not wait long enough for her to undress. She was not properly dressed, to begin with, but came wrapped in a light silk fabric, pure white and of the very sheerest weave. As Ruggiero caught her, a cloak slipped off her shoulders, and only that subtle veil remained. It did not cover the rose and lily of her flesh any better than glass would, and he took her through that. It was just as well. Ivy and the trees it victimizes do not grow more tightly than these two lovers did, sucking the very spirit from each other's lips, plucking flowers softer and sweeter than any seed can sprout in the scented sands of India and Arabia.

But of course the pleasure is indescribable. There is no point in my trying. It might be left to them to tell about; they often had more than one tongue in their mouths, and therefore might do better.

As it happens, these things were kept private in that place, or if not precisely private, at least passed over in silence. Alcina was like that, and her people knew— what they knew. Rarely is anyone blamed for keeping his mouth shut. At any rate, all these astute people offered Ruggiero their services and always made him most welcome among them. All bowed down to him and honored him. The infatuated Alcina willed it.

And life went on, with no pleasure left out, in that

resort of love. They changed clothes two or three times a day, now for one pleasure, now another, now for the pleasure of the change itself. They had no meals, but only banquets. There was a perpetual festival, with jousting, wrestling, theatrical exhibitions, bathing and dancing. Sometimes, near a row of fountains, in the shade of a row of artificial hillocks, they read aloud the amorous writings of antiquity. Sometimes they went hunting the timid rabbits through shady dells and over happy hills; or flushed the silly pheasants from the stubble with their dogs; or set snares or spread lime for thrushes amidst the sweet-smelling junipers; or troubled the fish in pleasant, secret places with baited hooks or nets.

Ruggiero lingered among all these delights and diversions while Charlemagne and Agramante struggled on. I don't want to disregard their story for his, nor to leave Bradamante who also struggled on, and in pain, and for him, lamenting the loss of her longed-for lover ever since she had seen him carried off, in such an unusual way, and without even knowing where. I will tell you about her before I go back to the others.

All that time, Bradamante went searching in vain through dark woods and sunny fields, through towns, cities, mountains and plains, never learning anything of her dear friend. She often went among the Saracen host, but she never heard a word about her Ruggiero. She asked more than a hundred people about him each day, and not one could give her any account of him. She went looking for him from camp to camp, in the tents and pavilions of the enemy. She could do this, freely passing among knights and foot soldiers, thanks to the ring that made her disappear when she put it in her mouth.

She did not give up; she could not and would not believe that he might be dead, for the fall of so great a man surely would be heard from the waters of the Hydaspes to the place where the sun goes down. She could not imagine where he had gone, but although she was utterly wretched, she went on searching, alone, in sighs and tears and bitter pain.

At last she decided to return to the cave where the bones of the prophet Merlin lay, to cry out and move even the stone to pity; for if Ruggiero lived, or if fate had indeed cut off his happy life, she would learn about it from Merlin; and then she would get advice of some sort, and follow it, for she could not think for herself beyond the one need to know the truth. So she took the road toward the forest near Pontiero, where the vocal tomb of Merlin was hidden in the mountainous and savage wild.

But the talkative sorceress—the one who had paraded her descendants and given her so much practical help in that fair tomb—had not forgotten Bradamante. That benevolent lady had always cared about the girl, knowing her to be the mother of invincible men, even demigods. Indeed, the enchantress wanted to know what Bradamante was doing every single day, so each day she had been casting lots to find out. For this reason, and without Merlin's help, she now knew how Ruggiero had been freed as planned and then lost, and she knew where in the East he had been taken. She had envisioned him on that steed he could not direct, since it was unbridled, going that perilous way as far as is possible on Earth. And she knew very well that he was staying there, sporting, dancing and dining in sweet leisure, not remembering his lord, his lady or his honor. The gentle knight could consume the flower of his best years in such idleness, and as a consequence be obliged to lose body and soul in one implacable moment; further, his reputation, the only thing that is left of us when the rest is gone, the only thing of a man's that can be kept alive out of the grave, might well wither or be cut off in the bud.

Fortunately that good sorceress cared for Ruggiero more than he cared for himself. She decided to lead him to the hard road of true virtue, in spite of himself—like a good physician, who cures with iron and fire and often with venom, who hurts at first, in order to save. She was not so indulgent, so blinded by excessive love, that, like Atlante, her heart was set only on keeping the young man alive. Atlante had raised him to be a warrior, but had come to prefer that Ruggiero live a long life, without fame and without honor, than that he miss even one year of easeful living. So the keeper of the hippogriff had sent Bradamante's beloved to Alcina's isle, there to forget war and good deeds in the pleasures of the court; further, as a master of the sum total of occult knowledge, practiced in all manner of spells, he had from afar snared the heart of that queen in a noose of love so strong that she would never be able to free herself, even if Ruggiero grew older than Nestor—that oldest Greek hero at Troy, who kept talking about the old days while they fought for Helen. (He did not make Ruggiero love Alcina, though; he knew that she would manage that herself.)

Now, returning to that good sorceress who knew so much, I maintain that she took the right road to meet the wandering, longing daughter of Aimone, Bradamante, on her way toward Merlin's tomb. Bradamante saw her, and her pain changed to hope; and the sorceress immediately told her the truth: that Ruggiero had been taken to—and by—Alcina.

The girl felt near death when she heard that her lover was so far away, and that he was not only in love but in danger besides—in danger, the sorceress pointed out, if a strong, quick remedy did not reach him. She comforted Bradamante and salved this new wound. She promised and swore to the girl that in a few days she would send Ruggiero back to her again.

"Since, lady," she said, "you have the ring that works against all spells and charms, I have no doubt that if I take it where Alcina keeps him, it will break hers, and then I will send your own sweet remedy back to you. I will leave early this evening and be in the Indies by daybreak." She went on, telling how she planned to use the ring to draw the dear loved one away from the soft, effeminate realm, and bring him back to France.

Bradamante took the ring from her finger; she would have given not only that, but her heart and her life as well, to help her Ruggiero. She gave the ring and all her hopes. She sent a thousand kisses to him. Then she took another road, toward Provence.

The sorceress went elsewhere, and just after sunset that evening conjured up a palfrey. It had one red foot. All the rest was black. I believe it was a demon like Dante's Alichino or his Farfarello, whom he mentions seeing in the Inferno, and that the enchantress called it from there in the form of a palfrey. Unbelted and barefoot, with her hair loose and horribly disheveled as usual, she mounted that thing, taking the ring from her finger in order not to impede her own magic. Then she flew with such speed that in the morning she found herself, as planned, on the island of Alcina, where the black horse faded away in the rising sunlight, only its red foot glowing until the sun was fairly high.

Meanwhile, the sorceress transformed herself wonderfully. She grew more than a palm in height, and made her limbs proportionately bigger; she grew and stopped at just the size that she thought was Atlante's, the necromancer who nourished Ruggiero with such great care. Then she sprouted a long beard. When it was long enough, she remembered to make it turn white. Then she made her skin darken and wrinkle. She knew that in expression, speech and manner, she could imitate old Atlante so well that no one could doubt her. So disguised, she spied on Alcina and her domain, until at last she saw the lovers separate. It took some days, because Alcina could hardly bear to be without that boy for a moment, but at last the sorceress had luck.

She immediately approached Ruggiero where he was enjoying a fresh, clear morning, beside a beautiful brook that flowed from a smooth hill toward a limpid little lake. His soft, delicious clothing, which Alcina had woven of silk and gold, with subtle, magic work, displayed his sloth and lust. A splendid necklace of rich gems hung from his throat to the middle of his breast. His once manly arms were both encircled by bright bracelets. His ears were pierced with fine gold wires, from which hung great pearls, greater than Arabia or India ever knew. His curly locks were damp with the sweetest perfumes. And all his gestures were languidly amorous, like those of one accustomed to serve proud ladies of Valencia as a slave. There was nothing sound in him but his name; all the rest appeared corrupt and rotten.

The good sorceress confronted him in the form of Atlante, with that grave, venerable face that Ruggiero always honored, with those eyes full of the wrath that the boy had once feared. And as she appeared, she asked, "Is this, then, the fruit of all my labor, all my time? Did I make your first baby food the marrow of bears and lions, did I teach you when you were a little child to go through horrid gorges, and into caverns, to strangle serpents, disarm panthers and tigers, and draw the teeth of wild boars, so that, after such discipline, you might be Alcina's Attis or Adonis? Have I wasted all my study of entrails, stars, and signs in conjunction? Were all those responses, auguries, dreams and visions in vain? For even when you were a baby they promised me that when you had reached this age, your feats at arms would be illustrious beyond compare!

"And this is really a great start! One could have hoped that you would make yourself into an Alexander, a Julius Caesar, a Scipio! Who, alas, could believe this of you—that you let yourself be Alcina's slave instead! And so that anyone can see it plainly, you're wearing around your neck, on your arms and all over, the chains with which she leads you captive, as she pleases.

"But if your own potential and the high deeds Heaven chose for you do not move you, oh, why deprive your successors of the good that I've predicted to you a thousand times? Why leave barren the womb where Heaven wills that you conceive the glorious and super-human issue who are to be brighter in this world than the sun? Oh, do not prevent the most noble souls formed as eternal Ideas from taking flesh, in the stock that must have its root in you! Do not prevent a thousand palms and triumphs, with which your sons, grandsons and successors, after hard deeds and evil wounds, will restore Italy to its primal honors!

"Just two of those souls that ought to blossom from your fruitful tree ought to move you: Ippolito of Este and his brother Alfonso. The world will not see many such as they from now until the Last Day, so excellent in the scale of virtues are they both! I could tell you

more about those two than about all the others together, though all ought to be brilliant, famous, invincible and holy. I have told you about them before.
It pleased you so to see that such illustrious heroes
were to be your descendants!

"And what does this creature you have made your
queen have, that a thousand other harlots lack?—she
who has been concubine to so many others. Have you
forgotten how happy she made them all in the end?
But, so you may know who Alcina is, without her
fraud and artifice, put this ring on your finger, and
go back to her and look—and see how beautiful she is."

Ruggiero was left ashamed and speechless, looking
at the ground, not knowing what to say. And as she
put the little ring on his finger, he recovered his senses
and felt such self-contempt that he wished he were
buried a thousand yards deep so that no one could
see his face. At that moment, of course, the sorceress
resumed her proper form. He saw the robe and her
feet change, and he looked up to see a stranger instead
of Atlante. (Incidentally, I forgot to tell you that her
name was Melissa.) She introduced herself to Ruggiero
and told him why she had come—sent by his beautiful
lady, who still loved him as before and could not bear
to be without him much longer—in order to free him
from the magic chains that held him. She told him she
had taken the form of Atlante of Carena to make him
listen to her, while he was still ensorcelled, and to take
the ring. Now that he had it, and was healthy, he ought
to see and understand everything.

"That gentle maid who loves you so much," she
said, "and who deserves as much love from you, and
to whom, if you'll remember, you owe your liberty,
sends you this ring that remedies all magic. And indeed
she would have sent her heart, if her heart had the

same power as the ring, for your health, safety and salvation."

She went on to tell him about Bradamante's love, and praised her worth as much as truth and affection allowed, using all the best rhetoric, befitting a wise messenger. Soon enough, she half-persuaded Ruggiero to hate Alcina almost as much as if he had already seen her plain. This is not so strange when you remember that his love was indeed forced by enchantment, and that the ring nullified that. Now, remembering Bradamante, he felt toward Alcina as one might toward a pretty painting when one has seen enough of it. And when, wearing the ring, he saw her face to face, he would realize that she never had had beauty. Her apparent beauty was merely magic, from toenails to scalp. The beauty was false; Alcina was scum.

Like a little boy who puts away a ripe apple, then forgets where it's hidden, and days later discovers his treasure all spoiled and putrid, so it was with Ruggiero after Melissa made him return to see the fay.

He found, instead of the beauty he had left not long before, a woman so repulsive that all the Earth had none who was older or more foul and deformed. Her face was ashen, wrinkled and emaciated. Her hair was thin, patchy, and white with age. She was only about three feet tall. All her teeth were gone, and all the rest was brown and wrinkled, for she had lived longer than Hecuba, longer than the Cumean Sibyl, and had not lived a virtuous life. But she used such art, unknown in our time, of course, that she could appear young and fair. Her art fooled Ruggiero and many others, all, or almost all, who ever set eyes on her, except a few as skilled in magic as she was herself. But with the ring, Ruggiero could read the cards correctly; it was no wonder that he lost all thought of loving, touching, even looking at her any more, now that he could see her truly, when her fraudulence could not avail her.

She smiled when she saw him, and held out her arms awkwardly, like a little crab.

But, as Melissa advised him, he did not show his feelings, simply pouted a little and said he wanted to try on his armor, neglected for so long. Then he armed himself from head to foot, just to see if he was still strong, he said, and not too fat and clumsy. And he took Balisarda, his sword, and hung it at his side; and also the miraculous shield that not only dazzled the eyes but left all enemies collapsed as though dead, and he hung it round his neck in the silk cover, as he had found it.

He went to the stables and had bridle and saddle put on a destrier blacker than pitch, again as Melissa advised him, for she knew how fast that horse was. It was Rabicano, and it had come with Astolfo on the back of the whale. Ruggiero could have had the hippogriff, too. It was tied right next to black Rabicano. But the sorceress, who was always at his ear, invisible, said, "Remember that he is too wild, as you know." She told him that the next day she would bring the hippogriff out of that country, and then at leisure he could learn how to bridle the beast and drive it on land and in air. If he took it now, he would arouse suspicion that he was getting ready to escape. Ruggiero did as Melissa wished, and left her.

Pretending to be going out to play, he rode out of the ancient whore's lascivious palace and approached the gate beyond which lay the road to Logistilla the good. There were guards. He attacked them suddenly, riding through them with sword in hand. He left some wounded, some killed, then went right on, across the bridge. Before Alcina had the news, Ruggiero was pretty far away.

In the next chapter, I will tell you what way he took, then how he came to Logistilla.

EIGHT

The Sacrifice of Angelica

Oh, how many enchantresses—enchanters, too—there are among us! They go unrecognized for what they are, making men and women their lovers by their arts, which transform their looks. They do not do it with spirits constrained by spells, nor with observation of the stars; they bind up hearts, in indissoluble knots, with simple pretense, lies and fraud. But whoever has Angelica's ring—rather, the ring of reason and judgment—would be able to see the true face of everything unobscured by art and lying. With that ring, some who seem beautiful and good to us would be deprived of makeup and magic and appear evil and ugly. It was Ruggiero's good fortune that he had the ring to expose the truth for him.

Pretending, as I said, riding armed on Rabicano to the gate, leaving some of the guards dead and others dying, crossing the drawbridge and breaking the portcullis, Ruggiero forged into a wood, but did not ride far before he met with one who served the fay.

This servant carried on his fist a ravenous hawk he flew for pleasure every day, over the fields or a nearby pond where there was always game. He had a dog as a faithful companion. He rode a nag not much adorned. He thought that Ruggiero must be escaping when he saw him coming in such a hurry.

So he asked him haughtily where he was going so fast. Good Ruggiero did not answer. At which the man, even more certain that he was running away, decided to stop him. Stretching out his left arm, he said, "What if I just stop you? If against this bird you have no defense?"

And he threw the bird into the air, and it beat its wings, and Rabicano would not go forward. Then the hunter got down from his palfrey and took off the bit. The horse ran at Ruggiero like an arrow shot by a bow, ready to kick and bite. The hunter came quickly after, as if the wind or fire, rather, were driving him. The dog was also eager, and, unwilling to be last, charged Rabicano as fast as a leopard after a hare.

Ruggiero would have been ashamed not to face them. He looked at the hunter, who came so boldly on foot, and saw he had no visible weapon except a stick suitable for teaching the dog to obey. Ruggiero waited, but disdained to draw his sword. The man came up to him and hit him, hard. At the same time, the dog bit his left foot, and would not let go. The unbridled nag turned and kicked Rabicano's right flank three times or more. Meanwhile, the bird of prey made innumerable tight circles round the heads of both horse and rider, and with its talons raked Rabicano and wounded him. It so frightened the destrier with its shrill shrieking that he could not obey either hand or spur.

Finally Ruggiero was forced to draw his sword, and in an attempt to stop this harassment, he threatened now the animals, now the villain himself, with edge or with point. But the hunter and his beasts became even more troublesome, and they still blocked the road. Ruggiero began to think that it was dishonorable of him to let them delay him any longer, anyway. He knew that if he stayed there much longer, Alcina would have her men at his back. He already heard trumpets, drums and bells sounding loud from the palace, and from closer, too, it seemed. But he still thought it would be a mistake to use a sword against a servant without arms, or against an animal. It seemed more expedient, therefore, to uncover the shield made by old Atlante. He took off the scarlet sheath. The shield was still working. The hunter, the dog and the horse collapsed and the bird's wings folded so that it, too, fell to the ground. Ruggiero happily left them all asleep.

Alcina, who meanwhile had learned how Ruggiero had forced the gate, killing a number of her guards, was overcome by grief. It almost killed her. She shredded the dirty rags she wore, and beat her already ruined face, screaming at herself for her stupidity. She also screamed at her slaves, ordering them to take arms and gather around her immediately.

Then she divided them into two forces. She sent one down the road that Ruggiero was traveling. The other she sent down to the port, into the ships and out to sea, darkening the water with so many hulls and sails. In her desperation, she went with her fleet, and was so frenzied with her desire for Ruggiero that she left her city without watch or guard; even the palace itself.

Melissa, who had stayed at her post, ready to free the men who were kept in misery throughout that wicked realm, took this convenient opportunity to examine everything at leisure. She burned images, broke seals, defaced certain signs and undid magic knots. The place lost its charm and became squalid. Then she hurried through the fields around the palace and the city, putting Alcina's earlier lovers back in proper shape. Alcina's garden and zoo became a surge of young men, now free to go. All of them followed Ruggiero's trail, to take refuge with Logistilla, and all arrived safely. From Logistilla's land they eventually returned to their homes in Persia, Scythia, India and

Greece; they went back to their own countries with a debt they could never repay.

First of all, Melissa restored the English duke Astolfo to his human form. His kinship to Bradamante, and Ruggiero's courteous pleas on his behalf, made Melissa go to him first. Besides pleading for him, Ruggiero had lent her the ring so that she could rescue him and the others more easily. So Astolfo was made a man again. And, after freeing all the others, Melissa was not satisfied until she had seen him recover all his arms, including that golden lance that drove anyone out of the saddle at the first touch. It had been Argalia's —Angelica's brother's—before Astolfo came by it, and it had earned both of them honor in France. Then, her task completed, Melissa mounted the Moorish necromancer's flying steed, and had Astolfo mount in the croup. They flew to Logistilla, arriving an hour before Ruggiero.

Ruggiero, meanwhile, had struggled toward the wise fay's country over the mountains, through thick thorn bushes, amidst boulders, from cliff to cliff in the empty, inhospitable wilderness, where descending was no easier than climbing. After great exertion, he came at fervid noon to a beach between the sea and the mountain. It was all exposed to the sun, and had been from morning to midday. It was scorched, naked, sterile and empty. The burning sun struck the nearby slope. The heat was reflected from rock and water. The air was like an oven. The sand seemed about to melt into glass. All the birds were quiet in what little shade could be found there; only the cicada, from the thorny, withered plants, deafened the whole shore with its monotonous beat. The heat, the thirst and the effort that it took to go down that sandy road were Ruggiero's oppressive, exhausting, and only company on that solitary shore.

But because it isn't good always to tell about one

thing, nor always to listen to one thing, I will leave Ruggiero in this heat and go to Scotland and find Rinaldo again.

Rinaldo was favored by the king, by his daughter and by the whole country. Having saved the princess from the vile calumnies of her unsuccessful suitor, Rinaldo was free to say why he had come there, how in his king's name he begged for help from the kingdoms of Scotland and England. A good ambassador, he added the most plausible reasons to Charlemagne's pleas.

The king immediately answered that he would help as much as he could. His power was at the disposal of Charlemagne and the Empire, and in a few days he would have as many knights ready as he could. If he were not too old, he said, he would be leading them himself. Nor would that consideration be enough to make him stay behind, if he did not have a son whose strength and intelligence deserved command, though he was not to be found in the country at the moment. He hoped his son would return while the troops were being mustered and find them ready to go. So he sent his treasurers throughout his kingdom, collecting horses and men, while others loaded his ships with provisions and ammunition.

Rinaldo went to England while the king was preparing for war, and the monarch courteously accompanied Rinaldo as far as Berwick, where Rinaldo's own ship was waiting. He was seen to shed a tear when Rinaldo boarded. A prosperous breeze was blowing in the stern, and Rinaldo called good-bye to everybody. The pilot loosed the cables for the voyage and they sailed easily to the place where the fair Thames joins the salt water. At flood tide, the sailors rowed upriver to London.

Rinaldo carried commissions, in letters countersigned

by Charlemagne and King Ottone of England, who was
with him in Paris, commanding that whatever infantry
and knights the kingdom could supply were to be
ferried across to Calais to help France and Charlemagne. The lord who occupied the throne in Ottone's
absence greeted Rinaldo of Aimone with as much
honor as he would have shown the king. Then he issued
orders, and set the day for all the forces of Britain
and its adjacent isles to meet near the sea.

Lord, I must try to perform like a good musician
on a subtle instrument, often changing chord and varying the sound, choosing now the solemn, now the
lighter note. While I have been catching up with
Rinaldo, I have remembered gentle Angelica, whom
I left escaping him. Now I want to pursue her story
for a while.

She had just met a hermit, you may recall, and had
anxiously asked how she could get to sea, because
she was so afraid of Rinaldo that she thought she
would die unless she put the sea between them. She
could not feel safe anywhere in Europe.

But the hermit detained her, because it pleased him.
Her rare beauty had fired his heart, warming him to
the marrow of his bones. He soon saw, however, that
she had little confidence in him, and would not hold
back for him. He goaded his ass but could not speed
him up; his mount was not much good at walking,
much less trotting, and would not make an effort to
extend himself.

Because she got so far ahead—a little farther and
he would lose her trail—the friar went back to his dark
cave and called up a throng of demons. He chose one
of them and told it what he wanted. It flew after
Angelica like a bat, settled on her courser's flank, bored
a little hole and drew itself inside. Her horse noticed

it no more than it would a fly. And like the clever dog used to chasing foxes or hares in the mountains, who sees his prey go one way and goes the other, seeming to scorn its trail, then at the pass has it in his mouth and tears it open, so the hermit, by a different road, will overtake the lady wherever she turns. I know what he has in mind—as I will show you later.

Angelica, suspecting nothing of this, traveled for some days, now fast, now slow. The demon was hiding in her horse, waiting, like a smothered fire that can flare up suddenly into such a blaze that it cannot be extinguished and can scarcely be escaped. When she had chosen a path beside the great sea that washes Gascony's shore, keeping her palfrey near the surf where the water made the sand firmer, the fierce demon roused itself and drove her horse into the water so fast, so far, that it was swimming before Angelica fully realized what had happened, and it was swimming out to sea. The timid damsel did not know what to do except hold herself firmly in the saddle. She could not make the horse turn by pulling on the reins. He swam frantically, ever into deeper water. She gathered up her skirt so that it would not get soaked, and raised her feet. Her hair flew disheveled over her back and shoulders as the playful breeze assaulted her. But all the major winds kept still, as if, with the calm waters, all were intent on her great beauty, watching, waiting.

She turned her eyes to the shore in vain, and could only weep, seeing the shore always shrinking.

Out of sight of land, the steed swam toward the right in a great circle. She scarcely noticed it had turned, at last, until she saw land again. But this was a different sort of shore: dark cliffs, full of darker grottoes, with night already beginning to blacken it utterly.

Her horse collapsed and drowned in the surf; she found herself alone, a moment later, on a little beach under the cliffs, by caves that frightened her at the mere sight, in the hour when Phoebus Apollo goes to rest in the ocean, leaving the earth and the air all dark. She could only kneel in the sand, so still that anyone who saw her would have been unsure whether she were a living woman, or one of stone, dark and wet from the waves—except the one who expected her there.

Dazed and motionless in the shifting sand, with her hair loose and disordered, her hands clasped together and her lips still, she moved at last only to raise her tired eyes to the sky. She stared at the stars that were coming out, as if accusing the Great Mover of turning everything against her. She seemed stunned for a while longer, then began to cry and speak.

"O Fortune," she said, "what more is there, before you are satisfied with me? What more can I lose to you, except my miserable life? But you don't want that! You won't take it! For you were quick enough to drag me out of the ocean again, though you easily could have ended my poor days there. So I suppose you want to see me suffer even more before I die. But I can't see how you can hurt me more than you have already. I have been driven from my royal throne. I cannot hope to regain it. I have lost my honor, too, and that is even worse. Although I did not sin, in fact, everyone says I did, because I am helpless, and wandering. What good can a woman expect in this world, when she loses her reputation?

"It has only hurt me—alas!—that I am young and considered fair. Whether I'm fair or not, I cannot very well thank Heaven for the gift, for this gift has caused all my troubles. My brother was killed for this, in spite of his enchanted arms. For this, King Agricane of Tartary destroyed my father Galafrone, though he was Great Khan of Cathay in the East, and I have come to such a state that I must change miserable dwellings from one night to the next. If possessions, honor and people you have taken from me, and done me all the ill that you could, what further pain do you reserve for me? If it was not your cruel sentence to drown me in the ocean, if that would not satisfy you, why not send some wild beast to devour me? Do not keep me longer in agony! No martyrdom could be so bad that I would not thank you for it."

Thus the lady was crying, when the hermit appeared close beside her.

He had watched her a long time from the very top of a spire of rock above. He had watched for her even while she was out at sea. He had come to this place six days before, carried by a demon. And now he had come down to her, feigning as much devotion as had those truly saintly hermits, Paul and Hilarion and Simeon.

When she first saw him, she did not know him and took some comfort; her fear ebbed away, little by little, though she did not quite recover and remained very pale. "Pity me, father," she said to him, "for I have come to the end; I cannot go on." And with her voice interrupted by sobs, she told him what he already knew.

He stopped her story to comfort her, murmuring suave and pious things, and as he spoke to her, he put his bold hands to her wet cheeks, and then on her wet breast. Then, feeling safe, he tried to embrace her.

Blushing with modesty and anger, she punched him in the chest so hard that she knocked him back against the cliff. She got up, ready to hit him again.

Too frightened to try to take her by force, he groped in the pouch he still carried at his side and took out a vial of some liquid. Unstopping the vial, he splashed its contents in her eyes, those eyes where flashed the greatest light that Love had ever made. The stuff had the power to make her sleep, and she fell recumbent in the wet sand at the rapacious old man's will.

He pounced on her, embraced her, and felt and handled her as he pleased. She slept and could not defend herself, and there was no one to see in that rough and deserted spot. He kissed her breast, he kissed her lips—but he found his steed too bowed down with age for riding. His weak flesh could not respond to his desire. It was too old and worn out, and he exhausted himself trying to rouse it. He tried every way he could think of, but the limp animal would not get up. He pulled on the reins and tortured it, in vain; he could not make it raise its head. And at last he fell asleep beside the lady.

Then another disaster fell upon her; Fortune seems never to give up when she chooses to mock a mortal.

Before I tell you about her next trial, I have to digress a little from my straight path. In the ocean, in the north and toward the sunset, beyond Ireland, lies an island named Ebuda, whose people are few—few on account of the sea beasts once sent by Proteus to avenge an insult and still troubling them.

Their ancient history relates, whether truly or not, that a powerful king once ruled the land and had a daughter so graceful and beautiful that when she showed herself on the seashore, she set Proteus on fire in the midst of the waters. One day the god found her alone, took her in a great wave, and left her pregnant. Her father was not pleased. He considered the matter very grave, and pious and severe as he was, he could neither excuse her nor pity her, and would not spare her life. Pride and Wrath can drive a man so far. And he would not stay the quick execution of the cruel doom for her pregnancy; he also put his sinless grand-child to death, before the child was born.

Proteus, who shepherds the wild flocks of Neptune, ruler of the waves, heard about his woman's mistreatment. In his own great wrath he broke the natural order of things: he did not hesitate to send up onto the earth his herds of sea beasts. They destroyed fields and crops, sheep and oxen, even farmhouses and their inhabitants; and often they went to the walled cities and besieged them from all sides. The people had to abandon their fields; night and day, weary and afraid, they stood armed against the monsters. At last, seeking some remedy, they went to consult an oracle: out of the city, up to the mountain, a dangerous mission until they reached the steepest slopes, on account of the monsters on the land. The oracle gave them this answer: they must find a damsel as beautiful as the other, dead one, and offer her at the edge of the sea to angry Proteus in exchange. If she found favor with him, he would leave her pregnant, or take her with him, and not come back to destroy them. But if she was not acceptable to him, he would not cease, and they must present him another, and another, until he was content.

So began the hard fate of all the prettiest women among them. Each day, one was taken to Proteus in the hope that he would find her pleasing. The first and all the others who followed her, day after day, from ancient times, died like the princess he had loved. All of them went to stuff the belly of that terrible sea monster, the great Orc, who still stayed close to the mouth of Ebuda's river after the rest of the atrocious beasts had left, unable to sustain themselves so long out of the water. Whether the part about Proteus was true or not (I don't really know, nor even whether everybody still believed it), the idea and the oracle's interpretation were the foundation of their ancient, cruel law against women, and they still observed it. The monstrous Orc came to the shore every day and was fed. Though it may be bad luck to be a woman in any land, in Ebuda it was intolerable.

Unhappy the damsels Fortune transports to that shore! The people of Ebuda always watched the sea, and were quick to make merciless sacrifice of strangers. The more from outside who were killed, the less their own numbers were exhausted. But because the wind did not always drive prey to them, they also went searching for women along other shores. They scoured the sea in pirate galleys, in brigantines, in every available craft, to gather relief for their torment from near and far. Many women they got by force, some by flattery, and others by gold. They always kept their prison towers full of foreign women.

Now one of their galleys, coasting by that lonely cove where the unfortunate Angelica was sleeping on the sand, put a couple of boats to shore to get wood and fresh water, or maybe they had some gold hidden in a grotto somewhere. And they found that flower of beauty and grace in the holy man's arms.

O too dear, too excellent prey for so barbarous and villainous a people! O cruel Fortune, who would believe that you have so much power in human affairs that you could consign, for a monster's meal, the great beauty for whom King Agricane led half of Scythia through the Gates of the Caucasus, into India, to die? The great beauty that King Sacripante placed before his honor and his own realm, Serican? The great beauty that made Orlando of Anglante tarnish his bright fame and good judgment? The unsurpassable beauty that held all the East in awe, and overturned empires! Now she had no one, she was alone. She was chained while she slept, and they carried the holy magician with her to the ship, which was already full of other sad victims.

They raised their sails again and were soon back at their evil island, where they shut Angelica in their strong fortress until the day it should fall her turn to feed their Orc. Her angelic beauty moved even those fierce savages to pity for a while; they deferred her death for many days; they preserved her for special need, pardoning her and sacrificing all others before her; but at last they had no others from elsewhere.

And finally they led her to the Orc, with all the people weeping after her. Who can describe the anguished wailing that pierced the sky? I wonder that the cold rock where they chained her, and where she waited helplessly for her abominable death, was not rent with pity. I can't, I won't try to go on; this hurts me so much that I am forced to turn elsewhere for some less tragic subject, until I can face this again. Surely the most wretched worm, the tiger blind with fury, even the venomous serpents who slither through the hot sands between the Red Sea and the Atlantic, could not have looked on, nor thought of, without grief, Angelica tied to the naked rock.

Oh, if only her Orlando had known! But he had gone to Paris to look for her, and Paris was besieged. Or if the two whom that clever old man tricked with a messenger from Hell had known! They would have followed her angelic steps through a thousand deaths to give her help if they had known! But what could they do now, even if they had news of her, when they were so far away?

Agramante, the famous son of King Troiano, had laid siege all around Paris. The siege was long, and the city came one day to such an extremity that it almost fell into the enemy's hands while it was burning fiercely; and if prayers had not appeased Heaven, which deluged all the plain with dark rain, the holy Empire

and the great name of France would that day have
fallen to the African spear. The almighty Creator had
turned his eyes to old Charlemagne's just complaint,
and with the sudden rain He put out the fire, which
human skill and labor might not have been able to
smother. It is wise to trust in God; no other can give
better help. The devout king knew very well that he
had been saved by divine intervention.

That night, Orlando in his weary bed was troubled
by his thoughts—thoughts that turned now here, now
there, could not be seized and never would be still,
like sunlight or moonlight in shimmering water, trapped
under a wide ceiling, leaping right and left and up and
down. His lady had come back to his mind (not that
she was ever really gone from it), and his heart burned
more fiercely than ever, though during the day, and
when he slept from sheer exhaustion, the fire seemed
to sink. But now he could think of nothing but the
lady who had come with him all the way to the West
from Cathay. And here he had lost her, and after
Charlemagne was routed near Bordeaux, he found no
trace of her. He was in agony over this, and vainly
repented his foolishness to himself.

"My sweetheart," he cried, "how vilely I behaved
with you! Alas, how much it bothers me that, able to
keep you with me night and day, when your goodness
did not deny it to me, I let them put you in Namo's
care! As if I didn't know better than to resist such
a wrong, or as if I didn't know how. And didn't I
have good reason to resist? Maybe Charles would not
have insisted then. If he had, who could have forced
me to give you up? Why didn't I take arms, ready to
let them take my heart out of my breast rather than
take you? But in fact, neither Charles nor all his men
were strong enough to take you from me by force.

"If only he had placed her under adequate guard,

in Paris or in some strong fortress! He must have given her to old Namo only so that I'd lose her like this! Who could guard her better than I? For I would guard her to my death, guard her more than my heart, my eyes. I should have done it, I could have done it, and yet I did not do it.

"Ah, where are you wandering now, without me, my sweet life, so young and so fair? Like a lost lamb, when the light is gone, straying among the trees and bleating, hoping to be heard by the shepherd, bleating until the wolf hears from far away, and the poor shepherd mourns for it in vain. Where are you now, my hope? Do you still wander alone? Or have the evil wolves found you without the protection of your faithful Orlando? And, that flower that could raise me to Heaven among the gods, the flower I always preserved intact, untouched, not to disturb your pure, modest spirit, alas! Have they reaped and spoiled it by force? Oh, misery! Woe is me! What can I do if they have plucked my fair flower, except die? Almighty God, make me suffer every other grief before that! For if that were true, then I must take my life with my own hand, and doom my desperate soul to Hell." Thus, sobbing and sighing, the afflicted Orlando spoke to himself.

Everywhere else, weary animate creatures rested their tired spirits, on feathers, on stone, on grass and in the trees. But you, Orlando, barely close your eyelids, stung by such piercing thoughts; your thoughts do not even let you enjoy such brief and fleeting slumber in peace.

For it seemed to Orlando that upon a green bank all painted with sweet-smelling flowers he saw the beautiful ivory and the native crimson that Love had brushed and blended with his own hand, and the two bright stars on which his soul fed, enthralled in the net of love; that is, the fair eyes and face that had stolen his heart from his breast. Seeing Angelica again, he felt the greatest joy, but then, behold, a storm came, destroying the flowers and bringing down the trees, such a storm as when the north wind, the south wind and the east wind all joust together. And it seemed that in order to find shelter, he went wandering in vain in a desert, and, not knowing how, lost the girl in the gloom. Then he rushed here and there, without thought of shelter, calling her name, but he did not find her. And when he cried out, "Woe! Woe! Woe! Who has turned my sweet into poison?" he heard the girl, weeping, calling for his help, entreating him by name. He went as quickly as he could toward the voice in the thick darkness, but he still could not find her. He went on searching and never found her. "What bitter agony," he said, "not to see the sweet rays of her eyes!" Lo, from another direction he heard another voice: "Hope to joy in them never more in this world!" At this horrible cry, he woke up and found himself wet with tears.

Without thinking that such apparitions may be false, especially when one dreams in fear or in desire, he now felt so sure that his love had come to shame and harm that he jumped out of bed like lightning. He hurriedly armed himself in plate and mail and took his destrier Brigliadoro. He did not want the services of any squire. And in order to be able to travel every road without blemishing his dignity, he did not take his own honored insignia, quartered, red and white, but chose a black shield to bear, maybe because it symbolized his pain. He had taken it from an obscure Saracen leader he'd killed a couple of years before.

He left silently, in the middle of the night, without a word to his uncle; he did not even say good-bye to his faithful friend Brandimarte, whom he loved so much.

But after the Sun shook out his golden locks, coming out of the rich mansion of Tithonus, making the damp shadows flee, the king learned that the paladin was not there. To his great displeasure, Charlemagne realized that his nephew had gone in the night, when he most ought to be there to help. The monarch could not contain his wrath. He complained aloud and loaded Orlando with words of reproach, threatening that if he did not return, he would be sorry for making such a mistake. Brandimarte, son of Monodante, who loved Orlando as he loved himself, did not wait. Whether hoping to make Orlando return, or distressed at hearing him criticized and cursed, he too left the city that evening.

Brandimarte said nothing to his Fiordilisa, because he did not intend to let her hold him back. She was his delight and they were rarely apart. She was beautiful, graceful, courteous and wise. And if he took no leave, it was only because he hoped to return to her the following day. But then things happened that kept him longer than he planned. After she had waited almost a month and did not see him again, she was moved by her desire for him to set out with no company or guide and to go looking for him through several countries, as the story will tell in the proper place. I shall not tell you more about those two now, because Orlando of Anglante is more important to me.

Orlando, after changing his shield, went right to the city gate and by saying to the captain of the guard, "I am the count," had him lower the drawbridge. He rode out at once, straight down the road that led to the enemy. What happened to him next is covered in the next chapter.

NINE

The Perils of Orlando

Love is cruel and treacherous and can do whatever he wants to a heart he has enslaved. Think of what Love has done to Orlando: Love drove out of his heart all the loyalty he owed to his lord. Before he loved, he was wise, respectful, and the faithful defender of the Holy Church; now, in love, he cared little for his uncle, little for himself, and less for God. But I, for one, find it easy enough to excuse him. It comforts me to have such company in my weakness. I, too, am weak and slow in following my good, but sound and brave in following my ill.

So Orlando deserted, all dressed in black, and thought nothing of abandoning so many friends; and he went into the enemy camp, where the armies of Africa and Spain were camped in the muddy fields, or rather uncamped, because the rain had scattered them far and wide, in groups of ten men, or twenty or fewer, to the shelter of trees and huts on higher ground. Almost all of them were sleeping, tired and worn out. In broken heaps they slept, and the count might have killed a great many of them, but he never drew Durindana from its sheath. Orlando was so generous and gallant that he would not stoop to killing sleeping men. Instead, he merely went searching among them, trying to find some news of his lady. Whenever he found a guard or anyone else who was awake, sitting up, watching, he described her, sighing, and asked

him if, by his courtesy, he could tell where he might
find her. And after daylight came, he searched the
whole Moorish camp. He could do this safely, in his
Arab disguise, with his knowledge of languages other
than French. (He had such facility in Arabic that he
seemed to have been born and raised in Tripoli when
he spoke it.) He did nothing for three days but inter-
view enemies for news of Angelica, all to no effect, all
without a single word of her.

Then he rode out of the camp, through the surrounding towns and cities, and searched not only the
kingdom of France, but also Auvergne and Gascony,
down to the smallest village. Then he searched from
Provence to Brittany, and from Picardy to the borders
of Spain. He began this quest at the end of October,
or the beginning of November, in the season when
we see the leafy dress stripped from the trembling
limbs of the trees and bushes, until they stand naked
in the cold, and all the small birds retreat in close
ranks to the south. He did not give up that bitter
winter, and he did not give up the next spring.

One day, going from one country to another, as he
did so often, he faced the river that divides Normandy
from Brittany. Ordinarily, it runs softly to the nearby
sea. But that spring it was flooded and white with foam,
from the snow that was melting in the mountains and
from heavy rains. And the flood had undermined the
bridge and had carried it away, closing the border.

He rode along the bank, looking for a place to
cross. It looked as if only fish or fowl could have made
it. Then, behold: a boat gliding toward him, with a
damsel sitting in the stern. He called her and she
steered toward him, but then held off, not letting the
wash carry the bow to the muddy bank, staying
clear of the shore, as if afraid of being put upon against
her will.

Orlando asked her to let him board, so he could cross the river.

And she called back to him, "No knight can cross unless he promises me, on his faith, to take part in the most honorable and just battle in the world. If you want me to help you cross to the other side, knight, promise me that before the end of next month you will go and join the King of Ireland, who is preparing a fair fleet in order to wipe out the island of Ebuda. Of all the lands the ocean embraces, Ebuda is the worst. You must know that Ebuda is one of the islands beyond Ireland. By law, Ebuda sends pirates to every shore they can find, to take as many women as they can, to feed alive to a greedy monster that comes to their shore every day. The monster is never disappointed. When the people of Ebuda cannot steal enough women, they buy them, the fairest to be found. You can see how many women are killed on Ebuda: one a day, for all these years. And if you have a shred of pity for womankind, if you are not wholly a rebel to Love, you should be happy to be among those who are chosen to go on such a useful quest."

Orlando barely allowed her to finish her story before he swore to be first in that mission. He could not stomach hearing of any evil, ugly deed, and on hearing of this one, he was inclined to think, then persuaded by fear to believe, that these people had taken Angelica.

This idea so possessed him that he forgot everything else and decided to sail for that evil island as soon as possible. Before the next sun had set in the ocean, he found a ship near San Malo, got on board, and took it over and had the sail raised. He passed Mont Saint Michel that night. Passing Breac and Landriglier on his left, he went along the coast of Brittany, then trimmed sail for the white cliffs that gave the name Albion to England.

But the south wind fell, and winds rose in the west and the north with such strength that the sailors had to lower all sails and turn the stern to the tempest. As far as the ship had come in four days, it was driven back in one. But the pilot was good, and kept the ship on the open sea, away from any shore, where it would have shattered like fragile glass in the wild surf. After four days of ferocity, the wind fell. On the fifth day, it was mild enough to let the ship enter the mouth of the Schelde, below the city of Antwerp.

As soon as the exhausted pilot got to shelter in the harbor, an ancient, white-haired man came down from a city on the right bank. He greeted them all, then turned courteously to Count Orlando, whom he took to be their captain, and asked him if he would be so kind as to come ashore to meet a damsel, whom he would find beautiful and also sweeter than any other in the world, or else be so kind as to wait for her to come and meet him at his ship. "Every knight who comes here does," he said; "not one, arriving at this harbor, by land or by sea, fails to converse with her, to advise her about the terrible trouble she's in."

Orlando had already jumped down to the shore without a moment's hesitation, being humane, compassionate, and full of courtesy; and he quickly followed the old man, only a little impatient with the delay.

The old man led him into the city, to a palace. On climbing the main stairs, Orlando met a girl in mourning—mourning which showed as much in her face as in her black dress and the black cloth hanging in the palace galleries, halls, and rooms. After giving him a pleasant greeting, she had him sit down, and then in a sad voice she told him her story.

"I want you to know that although I have been driven here, in the south, I am—I was—the daughter of the Count of Holland, who loved me so much (although I was not his only child, for I had two brothers), that he gave me whatever I wanted. He never said no to me. I was very happy.

"Then it happened that a duke came to our capital, the Duke of Zeeland, on his way to fight the Moors in Biscay. He was so beautiful—and I never had been in love before. It was not long before he took me prisoner. And I believed, from all appearances, and I am sure it is the truth, that he loved me and loves me sincerely. A contrary wind, contrary to others, not to me and not, I believe, to him, kept him with us for some time. Forty days, I think it was. It seemed a few moments to me; the time went so quickly. We were together often, talking, and he promised me, and I promised him, that when he returned we would be married with solemn rites.

"Bireno, that is my lover's name, you know, Bireno had just left when the King of Frisia, which is not far north of us in Holland, sent the worthiest nobles of his state to my father, to ask for me for his son, his only son, who was called Arbante.

"But I had given my word to my faithful lover, Bireno. I could not break my promise. And even if I could, Love would not let me be so ungrateful. I did not know the treaty was all but concluded, wanting only signature. To get my father to break off negotiations, I told him I would rather die than be given in marriage to the land of Frisia. My good father, pleased only when he pleased me, never wanting to disturb me, thereupon refused to sign.

"At this, the proud King of Frisia took such offense and conceived such hatred that he actually invaded Holland, beginning the war that has cost me all my family.

"Besides being strong and so powerful that few in

our age can compare with him, and being so clever
in his evildoings that he can make others' strength,
bravery and wit work against them, he has a secret
weapon that the ancient world never knew. Nor, except for him, does the modern world know it, either.
I understand that it is an iron harquebus, a hollow
tube of iron about two yards long. He stuffs it with
powder and an iron ball. Then, back where the pipe
is closed, he touches fire to a hole so small that one
can barely see it. Then the ball shoots out with such
a sound it is like thunder and lightning. Whatever
the ball hits is destroyed as if by a thunderbolt; the
weapon bursts through everything, knocks everything
down, smashes everything to pieces.

"Twice he routed our army with this device, and he
killed both of my brothers. The first, in his first attack.
The shot broke the breastplate and went right through
the heart. The other, in the other battle, or retreat,
because by then my brother was fleeing and was shot
from behind.

"Then, defending the only castle that was left to
him—he had lost all the rest—my father was killed
the same way. While he was going back and forth
on the wall, providing for this and that, the traitor took
aim at him from far away and shot him between the
eyes.

"So my brothers and my father were dead, and I
was the only heir to Holland, and the King of Frisia,
to strengthen his hold on the realm, told me and my
people that he would give us peace if I were now willing
to do what I had refused to do before: take his son
Arbante for my husband. Of course I refused again. It
was not only because I hated him and all his family, for
killing all of mine and for pillaging, burning, and ruin-
ing my country, but even more because I would not
wrong the man I had promised to marry when he re-

turned from Spain. 'For every evil I have suffered,' I answered the King of Frisia, 'I am willing to suffer a hundred more, and risk everything. I would rather be killed, be burned alive and have my ashes scattered to the winds, than do this.'

"My people tried to move me, protesting and praying to me to give him the whole country and myself, before my stubbornness ruined everything and everybody. But of course I still refused. So, after they saw that I would not be moved, they agreed with the Frisian and surrendered me, and my last city, to him.

"He did not hurt me in any way, and he assured me that I could live and keep my country, after all, if only I softened my will and married his Arbante. So I was forced to do it. I would have died to get out of it, but if I died without being avenged, I would have suffered for nothing. I thought it over a great deal and finally saw that, to my regret, the only thing that could help me was dishonesty. I pretended not just that it would not displease me, but that I longed for him to forgive me and make me his daughter-in-law. Then, among the men who had been in my father's service, I chose two brothers gifted with wit, courage and, even more, true loyalty. They had grown up at court, they had been with us since they were little boys, and they were mine; it would have seemed a little thing, to them, to give their lives for me.

"I told them my plan and they promised to help me. One went to Flanders to get a boat. The other I kept with me in Holland.

"Now, while the foreigners, and a few of my countrymen whom the foreigners trusted, were being invited to the wedding, it was learned that Bireno had assembled a fleet in Biscay in order to come to Holland. When the first battle was lost, when we were routed and my first brother was killed, I had sent a messenger to Biscay to give the sad news to Bireno. While he was getting ready to help, the King of Frisia conquered the rest. Bireno did not know that, of course. And he was sailing to help us. Having learned this, the King of Frisia left the ceremonies solely to his son, and put out to sea with his own fleet. He met my Duke of Zeeland; he smashed and burned his fleet, of course; and, as Fortune willed, he took him prisoner.

"But this news did not reach us, and I married the Frisian boy, and he wanted to lie with me as soon as the sun went down.

"I had hidden my faithful friend behind the curtains. He never moved, until he saw my bridegroom come to me; and then he did not wait for him to touch me, but stepped out and with a hatchet struck him a brave stroke on the back of his head. I would have cut his throat. I was ready to silence him with a pillow. But there was no need for that; he fell across the bed without a word, without a sound, after that one blow, like an ox in a slaughterhouse. So I killed the son, in order to spite the father, King Cimosco of Frisia, the most evil man alive, who had killed both of my brothers and my father and wanted me for his daughter-in-law, to subject our kingdom to his rule, and who perhaps would one day soon have killed me, too.

"Before there could be any trouble, we took whatever was worth most and weighed least, and my friend let me down to the water by a rope hung from the window and then followed very quickly. His brother was watching and waiting in a boat he had got in Flanders. We raised the sails to the winds, bent the oars to the water, and all three of us escaped, as it pleased God.

"I do not know whether the king was more grieved or enraged when he came back the next day and found himself so offended. He and his men came back so

proud of their victory and their capture of Bireno, and
expecting to join the wedding feasts, found everyone
in mourning instead. Grief for his son and hatred for
me never left him day or night, I am sure, but he
neglected the former and cultivated the latter. Tears
do not raise the dead, as I know. Revenge, on the
other hand, relieves one's hatred, enough, or more
than enough. He ought to have mourned for his son.
He did nothing but try to get his hands on me again,
to punish me. Immediately, all those known to be
friends of mine, or said to be, he declared guilty of
helping me, and he killed them or burned all their
goods. He would have killed Bireno to spite me, because I could not suffer for anyone else as much as
for him, but then he realized that if he kept him alive,
he could get me back.

"He did not kill Bireno; he gave him one year of
life to do whatever he could, by force or trickery,
through friends and relatives, to get me into that prison
in his place. The only way Bireno can save himself will
be by my death.

"Now I have done everything I can to save him,
short of losing myself. I had six towns in Flanders,
and I sold them, and spent all I got for them, trying
to corrupt the guards, and trying to persuade either
the English or the Germans to move against Frisia and
save my country and my love. Whether my agents
simply could not help, or did not do all they should
have done, they have given me words, words, words
and no help at all; and now that they have extracted
all my gold, they scorn me; and the year is almost at
an end, when neither force nor treasure can come soon
enough to spare my dear love from torture and death.

"For him, my father and my brothers died. For him,
I have lost my kingdom. For him, I have spent all
that was left to me, all that I had to sustain me, to

get him out of prison. There is nothing left to do for him but put myself in my enemy's hands, and free him. If, then, there is no other way, it will be sweet to me to give my life for his. But one thing frightens me: I do not know how to make terms so clear that I can be sure the tyrant will not cheat, after he has me. I am afraid that after he has me in prison, and can torture me as he pleases, for as long as he likes, until he lets me die, Bireno may not have his freedom, and be able to thank me for it, after all. That king is a perjurer, enraged, insane, and killing me alone might not satisfy him, and he might treat Blreno the way he will treat me.

"Now, the reason that I tell you all this, you and as many lords and knights as have come here, is only in order that, speaking with so many, someone might show me how to assure myself that after I go before that cruel king, he will not still keep Bireno. I am indeed afraid to die for him, if he will die after me anyway. I have asked some knights to go with me when I give myself up to the King of Frisia, and to give me their word that Bireno will be freed, so that when I am killed I may die content, because my death will have given life to my lover. But so far I have found no knight who can vow to guarantee this. None can promise not to let me be taken against my will if Bireno is not let go. All of them are so afraid of that weapon which no armor plate, no matter how thick, can withstand.

"But if you are as strong and brave as you look, and if you believe that you can take me to him, and also take me back if he deals crookedly with me, please go with me, for I shall have no fear, when you are with me, that my lord may die after I die."

Here the damsel stopped talking, and tried to stop crying, too. Orlando, whose will to do good never weakened, did not say much to her, because he never wasted words, but he vowed to her he would do more than she asked. He did not intend to surrender her to her enemy in order to save Bireno, but to save both of them, if his sword and his valor did not fail him.

They left that very day, since there was an even and favorable breeze. The paladin hurried in this quest, because he wanted to get it finished and go to the island of the sea monster. The good pilot steered the ship through the still estuaries, now this way, now that— west, then north, then east, up another river, to the islands of Zeeland and beyond. After three days of sailing, Orlando came to Holland and went ashore. But the princess did not go ashore with him; Orlando meant her to hear about the death of the evil King of Frisia, who had taken that country away from her, before she got off the ship.

He went ashore fully armed, riding a courser of brown—almost black. It had been bred in Denmark and raised in Flanders, and it was big and strong rather than light and quick. He had left his own destrier in Brittany when he sailed; that Brigliadoro, so fair and brave that he had no peer except Ruggiero's Baiardo.

He rode to Dordrecht, and found many armed men at the gate, for every prince is suspect in a new land, and this prince had more cause to be than most. Besides, news had come that a cousin of the lord kept imprisoned in Dordrecht had set out from Zeeland with an armed escort of ships and men.

Orlando asked one of the guards to go and tell the king that a knight-errant wanted to try him with lance and sword, but that he wanted to make a pact before they fought. If the king won, he could have the lady who killed Arbante, for he said that he had her nearby, and could deliver her into the king's hands. But he wanted the king to promise that if he lost, he would set Bireno free immediately and let him go his way. The soldier hurried to the king with this proposal; but the king, who knew neither virtue nor courtesy, turned his mind to trickery as soon as he heard it. He told himself that if he caught this knight, he would have the woman who had wronged him so much, too; granted that the soldier had understood properly, and that the knight really had the power to deliver her.

So the king had thirty picked men go to the gate where Orlando was waiting, but had them go in a roundabout way, in order to come up behind him. He instructed the soldier to parley with the knight until they arrived; when they did, he himself would appear at the gate with thirty others. As the expert hunter likes to surround the wood with big game inside, as the fishermen of Volana surround schools of prey with a long net, so the King of Frisia surrounded Orlando to prevent his escape. He wanted to take him alive, and thought he could take him so easily that he did not even call for the earthly thunderbolt with which he had killed so many, many people; he did not think of using it where he planned to catch, not kill. He imagined himself a sly fowler who keeps the first birds he catches alive, to attract more prey with their song.

But Orlando was not willing to let himself be taken at the first try. As soon as they formed their circle around him, he broke it. He lowered his lance, aimed where he saw the thickest crowd of soldiers, and rode; and he caught one, then another and another on the lance, like pastry on a spit. He speared six of them. The lance was not long enough to hold a seventh. The seventh man, nevertheless, was so severely wounded by the blow that he died, too. A good frogcatcher works like that, along the sandy edge of canals, moats and ponds; he gets them all together on a single spear, and does not have to remove them until the last has pushed the first all the way up the shaft to his hand. Of course, Orlando did not take time to remove his frogs; he simply tossed away the overburdened lance and began fighting with his sword. He drew that sword that never was drawn in error or in vain, and with each move Durindana made, cut or thrust, it disabled or killed another man, now one on foot, now one on horseback. Like a loaded paintbrush, everywhere it touched, it turned uniforms of blue, green, white, black and yellow to the same bright red.

By now, King Cimosco was sorry he did not have his secret weapon. He saw he needed it, after all. In a loud voice, with threats, he demanded it brought to him. But few men heard him, and none obeyed, for those who had retreated to relative safety inside the city were not eager to come out again. Realizing that all his men were fleeing, Cimosco himself hurried to the gate, and would have had the drawbridge raised, but even if that order had been heard, if would have done no good; Orlando was already over it, and after him.

The king turned, leaving Orlando lord of the bridge and the outer gate and the inner gate, too. And he fled up the street and passed all the others, thanks to the fact that his destrier was faster than any of theirs.

Orlando paid no attention to the rabble. Now, retreating, they were only in his way. He wanted to kill the king, not the others. But his own destrier prevented him from catching the king; it seemed to be reluctant, while the king's seemed to have wings. In a matter of moments, the king had disappeared from the paladin's sight.

But the king came right back to face him again, this time with a new weapon, for he had made his men bring out the hollow iron and the fire. He hid just around a corner, and waited, like a hunter in his blind, with his dogs in their spiked collars and his own long spear, waiting for the fierce wild boar who comes crashing down the hillside in the woods. The boar breaks branches and dislodges stones as he comes, like an avalanche or earthquake. So Orlando was preceded by all the people who fled from him in panic. And so Cimosco stood at his post to prevent the brave count from passing without paying for his pride.

As soon as Orlando appeared, the king touched the vent of the tube with flame, and it fired. In back, it flashed like lightning; in front, it spat thunder. The walls of that square shook, and the street trembled underfoot, and the sky reverberated with the blast, while the hot projectile, which shattered whatever it hit, sparing nothing and no one, hissed and screamed, but missed Orlando. Whether Cimosco was too quick, too eager to kill that lord, or his trembling heart made his hands tremble, too, or Providence willed that its faithful champion should survive, something made him miss.

The shot did disembowel the victim's horse, and it fell screaming, never to rise again. Both horse and rider fell to the earth, the one embracing it, but the other barely touching it. He got up again so quickly, so lightly, in spite of all his armor, it seemed as if his strength had grown by his fall. Just as the Libyan giant Anteus always rose from a fall even fiercer than before, because he derived strength from his mother, the earth, so Orlando seemed to rise, with doubled or redoubled force. And his shout of anger drowned out his dying horse's scream of pain. If you have ever seen lightning strike a magazine where carbon with sulphur and saltpeter are stored in some safe, hidden place, or a mere spark, scarcely touching the stuff, you know how it seems that heaven, not just the earth, explodes. Walls are shattered and heavy stones fly up to the stars. Then you can imagine what the paladin was like after he

struck the ground and rebounded with such ferocity,
a sight horrendous enough to make Mars shudder in
Heaven.

The King of Frisia twisted the reins in fear to turn
to flee. But Orlando was behind him, fast as an arrow
shot from a bow. And what Orlando had been unable
to do on his horse, he now did on foot. He ran so
quickly that no one who did not see it could believe it.
He caught up with the king almost immediately. He
leaped up with his sword out and divided the king's
body, down the spine, almost in two. The kicking corpse
crashed in the street, and the horse ran on, alone.

Lo! A new sound was heard in the city, a new clashing of arms, for Bireno's cousin and his men had come
from Zeeland, had found the main gate wide open and
had come inside. They found everyone in such fear
of the paladin that they could overrun the whole city
with little resistance. The city's captors and its captive
people fled, routed by any show of force, unable to
tell who these new invaders were or what they wanted.

But first one citizen and then another noticed the
dress and speech of the invaders, and realized they
were from Zeeland. Then they begged them for peace,
offering them carte blanche and telling their commander
that he could command them, too, to help drive out
the Frisians who kept Bireno in prison. The people of
Dordrecht always remained the Frisians' enemies, partly
because the King of Frisia had killed their former
lord, but chiefly because he was greedy, unjust and
cruel. Orlando, as friend of both sides, helped them
make peace together. Then their united forces left
not a single Frisian in the city untaken, or alive; they
killed or caught every one.

And they threw down the prison gates without looking for the key. Bireno thanked the count effusively.

With a great crowd behind them, the two men rode from the prison to the ship where Olimpia was waiting, Olimpia, the rightful ruler of that land, who had not dared hope that Orlando might do so much for her, since she had thought it would be enough if she alone were put in mortal danger to save her bridegroom's life.

All the people revered and honored her, and it would take long to tell how much Bireno caressed her, and she him, and what thanks both of them gave the count. The people raised her to her father's throne and swore fidelity. She, chained eternally to Bireno by Love, gave him the rule of her state and herself. And he, concerned with another matter for the present, left the rule of all the land and its fortresses in his cousin's hands. For now he planned to return to Zeeland, taking his faithful consort, Olimpia; and then, he said, he wanted to go on, into the kingdom of Frisia, to try his luck there. He thought his luck would be good, because he held a pledge to assure his taking of Frisia, and he considered it sufficient: it was the daughter of the King of Frisia, who had been found among the Frisian prisoners in Dordrecht. And he said that a young brother of his would have her for his wife.

The Roman Senator Orlando left Holland the same day he freed Bireno. He refused to touch anything among all the spoils he had earned except that war machine that resembled a thunderbolt. People wondered why he wanted it, since he did not need it, and Bireno was not happy about his taking it, but could not object. Orlando's reason was not his own defense, of course. He always considered it a weakness to go into any enterprise with an artificial advantage over others. Rather, he took it away in order to dispose of it where it never would injure anyone again, and with the thing itself he also took the powder and the balls and the flint and the fuse.

Once he was sailing over deep water, out of sight of land on any side, he took the thing and said, "So that never again may a knight fail in bravery on account of you, so that never again may the wicked brag that they are better, here you stay. O damned, O abominable machine, manufactured in the Tartarean deep by the malignant Beelzebub, who intended to ruin the world through you, to Hell, where you came from, I send you back again." And, saying this, he threw it over the side into the dark ocean.

Meanwhile, the wind kept the sails full, driving the ship steadily on its way toward the evil island of Ebuda. The paladin was eager to know if his lady might be found there, the lady he loved more than the whole world. He felt he could not bear to live another hour without her. He was afraid that if he stopped in Ireland, where a force was assembling to move against Ebuda, he might lose more time in some new adventure, and might have to say, later, in vain, "Alas! that I did not hurry!" He was so eager to get to Ebuda that he did not permit the ship to touch any other shore on the way.

But now we let him go where he is ordered to go by the naked archer who wounded him in the heart. Before I tell you more about him, I want to go back to Holland, and you may come with me. I do not want to disappoint you, and miss the wedding of Bireno and Olimpia.

Well, their wedding was fair and sumptuous, but not as sumptuous nor as fair as the feasts they will have in Zeeland, they say. But I must disappoint you about that. Those feasts will not take place—prevented by other events, which you will learn about in my next chapter.

TEN

The Shield of Atlante

Among all the faithful lovers ever tried through pain and joy and found constant, I give first place, not second, to Olimpia. No matter who might disagree, I still say that truer love than hers could not be found in ancient or modern times. And she had made her Bireno sure of her with so much proof that no man could be surer; she had proved herself as certainly as if she had cut open her very heart to show it to him. What better proof could she give him, or anyone give any man? And if faith and devotion deserve love in return, I say that Olimpia deserved even more love from him that he had for himself. He ought not to have left her for another woman, not even for Helen, the woman who brought so much woe to both Europe and Asia, nor even for a woman more beautiful than she. Rather than lose Olimpia, he ought to have lost his sight, forever, and hearing and speech and taste and life and fame, or something even more precious than these. If he loved her as she loved him, if he was as faithful to her as she was to him, or if he was ungrateful, even cruel, I will tell you now, and make you raise your eyebrows with wonder.

And after you have seen the bitter reward he gave her for all her goodness to him, ladies, you will never trust a lover's promises again, I hope. To get what they want, without considering that God hears and sees everything, lovers may weave promises and vows that scatter to the winds after they have slaked the avid thirst that burns them. Remember this example, and be a little less ready to believe their prayers, their tears. It is better to learn to be wise at another's expense, dear ladies. And watch out for the ones in the flower of their youth, with their faces still smooth, because their appetites are born and die like fire in straw. The hunter follows the hare in the cold, in the heat, along the shore and into the mountains, and thinks nothing of it after he takes it, and goes on only after one that flees, and these youths are like that. While you are hard to get, they love you, revere you, and serve you faithfully; but as soon as they can brag about the conquest, you are not a mistress but a servant, as far as they're concerned; they turn their false love from you, to another. I don't mean, don't love. It would be wrong to forbid it. Without a lover, you would be like a vine neglected in the garden, with nothing to cling to. I only warn you to avoid the boys with the first down on their cheeks. Pluck fruit that is not so hard and bitter, as long as it is not too ripe, or overripe.

I have told you that they had found the late King of Frisia's daughter among the prisoners, and that they said she was to be given to Bireno's young brother in marriage. Actually, Bireno himself had a taste for her, and he thought it would be a stupid courtesy not to indulge his taste and spare her for the boy—she was so delicate and helpless. Only fourteen, she was fresh and fair as a rose just budding in the spring sunlight. His love blazed up like fire set in ripe grain as soon as he saw her crying about her dead father, and the love Olimpia had ignited in him was extinguished by those younger, fresher tears. He suddenly felt so tired of Olimpia that he could barely look at her, and he felt he would die if he could not satisfy his lust for the other girl.

But until the day he was ready to satisfy himself, he restrained himself, and pretended to adore Olimpia still, and want only what pleased her. And if he caressed the other one (for he could not keep his hands off her), nobody suspected him; his caresses were ascribed to pity; to comfort one whom Fortune has thrown to the bottom of her wheel, to console the bereaved and afflicted, never was considered a fault, generally, but more often a great virtue, and the girl was very young and innocent. O Almighty God, how often human judgment is clouded! All Bireno's evil intentions were considered charity.

The sailors put their hands to the oars. The ship soon left the safe shore behind. The duke and his company skimmed over the salt water toward Zeeland. And all too soon they lost sight of the coast of Holland, because they were bearing more to the left, closer to Scotland, in order not to pass close by Frisia. And then a wind came upon them and sent them wandering for three days on the open sea. They came to shore on the evening of the third day, to an uncultivated, uninhabited island.

As soon as they anchored in a little cove, Olimpia went ashore, and there she dined with the unfaithful Bireno. She suspected nothing, and she was very happy. Then they went to bed together in a tent that the sailors had pitched for them in a pleasant spot. Everyone else went back aboard the ship for the night. After three days without sleep, afraid of the violent waves, now safe on dry land, far from their roaring, in the quiet grove with her love beside her and no care to trouble her, Olimpia slept very well; bears and dormice could not have slept more soundly.

But Bireno, busy with his deceitful thoughts, did not sleep. He lay awake beside her, without moving, until he knew she was asleep. Then he slid out of bed very quietly, made a bundle of his clothes, not risking the time to get dressed, and slipped down to the shore and his ship. He woke up his men without a sound, and without a sound they raised anchor and slipped out to sea, soon leaving the island and the sleeping Olimpia far behind.

Olimpia slept on and did not stir until the wheels of Aurora's chariot scattered frost on the ground, and halcyons began singing at the shore, lamenting their ancient misfortune. Then, neither asleep nor awake, Olimpia reached out to touch Bireno. She moved her arm, and then her leg, and then turned over, and felt only the cold sheets. Fear woke her up. She opened her eyes and did not see him. Immediately, she got out of bed, hurried out of the tent, and saw no one. She ran down to the harbor, her hands to her face, already suspecting what had happened. Coming to the edge of the water, she was certain, for although the sun was not up, the moon was shining, and she saw the cove was empty. Nor could she see anything out on the sea, where morning was brightening. Then she tore her hair and beat her breast and called Bireno, and the only answer was his name echoed from the pitying cliffs around the cove.

At the mouth of the inlet stood a high rock, carved out by the waves so that it was hanging far over the sea. Olimpia scaled it quickly, without thinking of the difficulty or the danger, and from the summit she saw, or thought she saw, for the air was not yet very clear or bright, the full sails of her lord's ship, fleeing, far away. Not until then did she collapse, her face turning white and cold as snow, her body motionless where she lay at the edge of the cliff. After awhile the rising sun warmed and roused her. Raising her head, she stared out to sea, though she could no longer see anything in the glare, and she called as loudly and as often as she could, "Bireno!" She beat her hands on each other and on the stone. Tears ran down her face. She moaned, "Where are you going, so quickly, so cruelly? Your ship does not carry its proper cargo. Let me go, too. You have my soul. Can my body be such a burden?"

And then she climbed to her feet and signaled madly with her robe, though she could not see the ship. The wind that had carried away her love was strong. It made her hair and her robe flutter like banners. It made white water on the sea. It drove Bireno on, farther and faster. And it tore away her tears and her cries and tore the robe out of her hands at last. She climbed down after it, slowly. She waded out for it, in the still waters of the cove. She thought of drowning herself, and went back to the beach and waded out again twice more.

Then, shivering and sobbing, she went back to the tent and threw herself face down on the bed, saying, "Last night we were two, together, here. Why am I left alone, widowed? O treacherous Bireno! Oh, the day I was conceived was cursed! What should I do? What can I do, here, alone? Who will help me? Alas, who will comfort me, now, ever? There is no one here, no trace of man on this little island, no ship I could board to escape. I will die of hardship. There will be no one to cover my eyes and bury me, unless the wolves of the forest dispose of my body. Oh, I must live in fear until I die! I'm already seeing bears, lions, tigers coming out of the woods with their sharp teeth and their claws. But what could wild animals do to me except kill me? To kill me once, I know, would be enough for them; and you, you make me die a thousand deaths, leaving me like this.

"But suppose a ship were to come, right now, and its captain pity me and take me away, anywhere I want to go, to save me from the wolves and hunger and the cold. Would he take me to Holland? You have the harbors and the forts! How could I go back to the country where I was born, when you have already taken it away from me, by fraud? You have taken my kingdom by fraud, by pretense of friendship, love, marriage. Oh, you were quick to bring all your men there, so you could hold it. And will I go to Flanders, where I sold the rest of my property to help get you out of prison? Woe is me! Where will I go? There is no place for me! Should I go to Frisia, where I could have been the queen, but refused, for you, for the ruin of my father, my brothers, everything. I would not reproach you for what I did for you. You know it very well. But now, look at the reward you've given me.

"Or suppose pirates come, to take me and sell me as a slave! Oh, before that, let the wolves come, and all the other wild animals, to crush me in their jaws, to tear me to pieces, to drag me to their dens!"

Keening thus to herself, she tore her face and her hair, and ran down to the water again. With her hair flying, she seemed frantic, possessed, and possessed not by one demon alone but by tens. Like Hecuba when she found her last son drowned, Olimpia raved at the edge of the sea. At last, hoarse and exhausted, she sat huddling on a rock, staring out to sea, unmoving until she might have seemed of rock herself.

But I have to leave her there in her woe, because I want to tell you about Ruggiero, too.

Ruggiero, tired and weary, traveled along another shore in the most intense heat of midday. The sunlight struck the hillside and the sea and was reflected back again. Under his horse's hoofs, in the only shadow, the fine, crumbling white sand seemed to boil. There was no stretch of wet sand for firmer riding; the sea was so smooth, the waves were mere ripples. And his armor felt as hot as it must have been when forged.

As I have said, his thirst and the labor of riding through the deep, hot sand on that solitary, open shore were bad enough company; but then, ahead, he saw a squat, ancient tower rising out of the water near the beach; a boat idled beside it. And when he got there, he found three females from Alcina's court in the narrow strip of shadow by the water. He knew them by their dress and by their manner. They seemed to be enjoying themselves; they looked fresh and cool, lying in the shade on rare Persian carpets, surrounded by sweet meats and bottles of wine. It was their boat that was moored at the tower, as if they were waiting for some light breeze to come and stir the sail, which hung flat against the mast. There was not a breath of air, and the boat was not even rocked by waves.

These creatures began speaking sweetly to Ruggiero, as he rode on his slow way over the uncertain sand, with his face and hands covered with sweat, his lips parted, his mouth full of thirst. They told him not to keep his heart so set on his errand, whatever it was. He ought not to mortify his poor body. He really ought to rest in the shade, where it was cool. But he paid no attention to them.

Two of them got up, gracefully. One glided over to his horse and put her hand on the stirrup, to help him dismount. The other held up a crystal goblet full of sparkling, foaming wine, to make him thirstier. The third merely looked very inviting, lying there. He wondered what they would look like if he were wearing the anti-magic ring, and he rode on. He was not going to dance to their tune. He reminded himself that any delay would give Alcina's forces more time to catch up with him. He looked back along the shore and saw no one riding after. Out at sea, he saw the long, dark line of a gathering storm. He wished it would come, and bring cool rain.

And indeed the sea does not rage so violently when a whirlwind descends on it, nor do saltpeter and pure sulphur explode so quickly when touched by a spark, as those three ladies blazed up with wrath when they saw Ruggiero ride on, safely, down his narrow path in the sand, scorning their beauty.

"You're no gentleman! You're no knight!" they yelled as loudly as they could. "You stole your armor!" "That warhorse can't be yours, either!" "Not by right!" "Only by theft! So I say you ought to be punished!" "By death!" "It's true!" "I'd like to see you hanged!" "Quartered!" "Burned at the stake, you ugly robber!" "You proud, vile ingrate!"

The loudest of the three went on abusing him with even more profligate insults. Ruggiero never answered. He could not hope for honor in that kind of competition. When they realized he was not going to turn around, all three splashed out and jumped into their boat. Two of them took the oars and rowed around the tower, and then along the shore as close and as fast as possible. The third went on shouting at him from the bow, shaking her fist and making other gestures at him as she cursed, threatened and insulted; she knew an insult for everything. They never quite caught up, but he could not altogether outstrip them. Beyond them, he could see the whole horizon darker, closer, less like a great storm rushing in on that unbearable calm and glare than like another shoreline.

But ahead, the beach widened, the cliffs sank away until there was only a line of boulders to his left, and then there was only flat, firmer sand and he was on a bar, at the strait dividing the part of the island Alcina had usurped from Logistilla's rightful realm. Across the strait were green hills and a crystal city. There were real waves and a cooling breeze. Alcina's creatures stopped rowing and drifted out to sea. A bigger boat was coming to meet him, piloted by an old man who must have been forewarned and waiting only a little distance offshore.

If you can judge the heart from the face, the old man was wise and good. Anyway, he was happy to take Ruggiero and his horse aboard and ferry them across the strait to the better shore. Ruggiero dismounted in the shallow water, jumped aboard and led his horse after, then jumped back into the water to push the boat from the sand, thanking the pilot and God for this help.

While they sailed over the blue waves, the experienced old man praised Ruggiero for his unprecedented wisdom in deserting Alcina before she gave him the magic cup she had given, at last, to all her other lovers. He also praised him for turning to Logistilla's land, where he would find holy customs, eternal beauty and infinite grace—nourishing the heart, never cloying. "The first sight of Logistilla," he said, "strikes wonder and reverence to your very soul. Then contemplate her noble presence, and everything else seems worth very little to you. Her love is different from the other fay's. In the other's love, hope and fear wear you out. In hers, desire doesn't beg for more; you're happy just seeing her. She will teach you things much more pleasant, in the long run, than singing and dancing, bathing and dining. She will teach you how to think, how to build ideas on firm foundations, and then they can soar like hawks in the sky, and then you can taste, in part, the glory of the blessed in your mortal flesh."

He was going on like this, and they were far from either shore, when he stopped. Ruggiero looked back, and saw the trouble for himself. Now that line was not a great storm or a distant shore, but a fleet of innumerable ships, and with her whole fleet, Alcina herself was coming, risking the ruin of her state and her own person in order to get back the sweet thing she had lost. Love moved her, but so did wrath. She had never been so indignant since the day she was born. Nothing had ever eaten at her heart like this.

Now she could see Ruggiero's face. She had the drummers beat faster, making the slaves at the oars work faster than ever before. The water foamed between all her ships and against either shore; her fleet almost filled the open water, like a solid wall. And Ruggiero could hear the sound of the drums and the sound of the sea, a great incoherent thundering, echoed back from the barren cliffs on one side and the green hills on the other.

"Ruggiero," said Logistilla's pilot, "uncover the shield—or you're killed, or shamefully taken prisoner."

Before he had finished speaking, Ruggiero had torn the cover open, making the shield's magic splendor shine over the water and along the whole line of ships, blinding the enemy. Everywhere it struck, brighter than the sunlight, men fell from the rigging to the decks, and from the decks into the sea, where the oars were rising, falling, fouling each other and splintering.

At the same time, watchmen on Logistilla's towers had rung the bells to signal her artillery, and from that shore, on either side of the harbor, the artillery fired like a storm. The shot began falling into the enemy fleet a moment after the light of the shield first reached it. So, at the last, help came from that side, too, to save Ruggiero's life and liberty.

Logistilla sent four ladies to greet him at the harbor: brave Andronica, wise Fronesia, honest Dicilla and chaste Sofrosina, who came first, shining like a star. Behind them, a matchless army marched down from the castle and lined up along the beach. And out of the tranquil harbor sailed a huge fleet ready for battle. So began another war, but this one was almost over. Alcina had not landed, but she was to lose all she had taken from her sister before. Many battles fail to end as expected.

Alcina not only failed to get back her fleeing lover, but of her entire armada, so many ships that the sea scarcely held them, only one little boat escaped the wreck and conflagration. Alcina was on it. She fled, and her miserable slaves stayed behind to be drowned, burned or taken prisoner. She knew she could not hold the land she had stolen long ago. But she felt the loss of Ruggiero most of all. Night and day she grieved bitterly over that loss. Night and day she cried real tears for him. And often she cried because she was unable to end her pain by dying, because she was unable to die at all. No fay can ever die while the sun revolves in its orbit and the stars keep their places. Otherwise, her pain might have been enough to move Clotho, the Fate, to cut the thread and end her life. Or she would have ended it herself, like Dido or Cleopatra, with a knife or the bite of a poisonous snake. But fays can never die.

We return to that knight worthy of eternal fame, Ruggiero, and leave Alcina in her eternal woe. Now I must tell you that after he was led out of the boat, on the safer shore, thanking God for his escape, he hurried over the firm dry land and up to the fortress that stood on the hills.

Mortal eyes never have seen, and never will see, a stronger or fairer citadel. Its walls were made of stone more precious than diamond or carbuncle. Stone like this does not exist, here below, and anyone who wants to see it must go where Ruggiero went, because I do not believe it can be found anywhere else, except maybe in Heaven. What distinguishes it from other gems, apart from its superiority, is that if a man looks into this one, he sees not only his form reflected, but his very soul, sees his own vices and virtues exposed, or expressed. Looking at himself in the bright mirroring surfaces, he sees himself truly, knows himself, and grows wiser; he will not fall for false praise or false blame, either. Moreover, the clear light of this stone imitates the sun, shining so brightly that whoever has such stone, wherever he is, can make daylight whenever he wants—like it or not, Phoebus Apollo, you jealous god.

The stone itself was not the only wonder there; the material and the workmanship so competed in excellence that it would be hard to judge which were better, nature or art. On the huge columns and arches, which seemed to support the sky when you saw them from below, grew gardens so spacious and fair that it would have taken incredible labor to cultivate them even on some well-watered plain. You could see these sweet-smelling shrubs and trees, lush and green, flowering and bearing fruit, all year round among the luminous towers. Elsewhere, roses, violets, lilies, amarinths and jasmines appear in one season, when they are born, live, and die withered and drooping on the stem. Everything is subject to the variations of the heavens, elsewhere. But there, the beauties of green leaf, fruit and flower were perpetual. It was not because nature was so temperate and kind to them on that island, but because Logistilla, with her own study and care, without paying heed to celestial motions, and impossible though it may seem, kept springtime fast, forever.

And there Ruggiero met her, in her garden in the sky. She was very happy to see him, pleased that so gentle and noble a knight would come to visit her. She ordered all her subjects to honor him like Astolfo. He was also at her castle, having arrived some time before, and Ruggiero was glad to see him, too. The last of all the others transformed by Alcina and reformed by Melissa came a few days later.

After a couple of days of rest, Ruggiero went to petition the wise fay with Duke Astolfo, who wanted to see the West again as much as he did. Melissa, who had come to the Indies by magic, but had no magic power to transport the others, spoke for both of them, and humbly begged the fay to favor, advise and assist them to go home.

"I will think about the best way," said Logistilla, "and in a few days I will be able to help you."

She soon decided that the flying steed should return Ruggiero to the shores of Aquitaine; but first, she wanted to make a bit for its great beak, so that the knight could restrain it and direct its course. Then she took the time to test it herself, then to show him how to make the creature soar on high, and how to make it fall, how to make it veer and circle, faster or slower, and hover on the wing. Ruggiero became master of that steed, learning how to ride it on high as a knight rides a good destrier on solid ground.

When Ruggiero was all ready, he took leave of the noble fay, whom he would love always, and he left her country. First I will tell you how it went with him, quite easily. Later I will tell you how the English knight took much more time and effort to return to Charlemagne and his friendly court.

Ruggiero did not fly back the way he had come, before, against his will. On that occasion, the hippogriff had carried him over the water and he seldom saw land below. But now, able to make it fly wherever he wanted, he decided to return another way. The beast had brought him from Spain to the east of Asia, in a straight line. Now he wanted to go on, to complete the circle he had begun, in order to have revolved around the whole Earth like the sun.

So he flew west, and saw Cathay and Manji with its

great city, Kin-sai. He flew over Himalaya and passed
Serican on his right hand. From Hyperborean Scythia
to the Hyrcanian Sea, he came to the lands of Sarmatia
and Turkestan, to the border of Europe. He flew over
Russia and Prussia and Pomerania. And although he
had every intention of returning quickly to Bradamante,
he enjoyed this journey so much that he wandered a
little. He saw Poland, Hungary, Germany and the
horrid lands of the north, and he came at last to England, off the western shore of Europe.

Do not assume, lord, that he saw all this in one
flight. He descended every night, somewhere or other,
and took the best lodging he could find, if he could
find any. Flying was so novel and wonderful that he
spent many days seeing land and sea from high above.

He came to London one morning and swooped down
over the Thames. In fields and over hills beside the
river, he saw innumerable men-at-arms. He would not
have noticed them from that height if there had not been
so many on horseback and on foot, marching to the
sound of drums and trumpets in ranks and files before
Rinaldo. If you remember, I told you before that
Rinaldo had come to England to get help for Charlemagne. Ruggiero arrived just as Rinaldo was reviewing
the troops outside London.

To find out what was going on, Ruggiero landed and
asked an English knight about it. The knight was friendly, and told him that there were companies not only
from England, but from Scotland and Ireland and all
the adjacent islands under all those banners. He told
him that when they finished this review, they were going
to march to the harbor, where a fleet was anchored,
ready to take them all across the Channel. He added
that the besieged French were living in hope of their
coming to save them.

"And if you want to be fully informed," said the English knight, "I will point out all the men for you.

"You see that big flag spilling in the breeze there, the one combining fleurs-de-lis with the leopards? That is the grand captain's standard, and all the others follow. His name is famous around here. He is Leonetto, the flower of the brave, the master of craft and ardor in warfare, the nephew of the king, the Duke of Lancaster.

"The one next to that royal gonfalon, blowing toward the hills, a green field with three white wings, is borne by Richard, Count of Warwick. The Duke of Gloucester's is the other one, with two antlers of a stag and half its forehead. The Duke of Clarence's is that torch. That tree is the Duke of York's. You see the lance broken in three pieces? That is the Duke of Norfolk's banner. The thunderbolt is the good Count of Kent's. The griffin is Pembroke's. The Duke of Suffolk has the scales, there. Now, you see that yoke with two serpents? The Count of Essex carries that one. And the garland on the azure field is Northumberland's. The Earl of Arundel has the boat sinking in the sea.

"There goes the Marquis of Berkeley and the Earls of March and of Richmond. Berkeley's the one with the cleft mountain on white. The second has the palm tree; the third, the pine standing in the sea. That one is the Earl of Dorset, and the other is Southampton, the one with the chariot, the other with the crown. Raymond, Earl of Devon, bears that falcon spreading her wings over her eyrie. The Earl of Winchester has the yellow and black; Derby, the dog; Oxford, a bear. The crystal cross you see there is the rich Bishop of Bath's. Look, that shattered throne on the gray field: Earl Ariman of Somerset.

"The knights in armor and the mounted archers number forty-two thousand. There are twice as many men on foot, give or take a hundred. As for those flags, the gray, the green, the yellow and the one striped with sable and azure, Geoffrey, Henry, Herman and Edward are leading infantry, each with his standard. The first is Duke of Buckingham. Henry has the county of Salisbury. Old Herman is lord of Abergavenny. And Edward is Earl of Shrewsbury. All these camped on the east are English.

"Now turn west, where you can see thirty thousand Scots led by Zerbino, their king's son. You see the great lion, between two unicorns, with the silver sword in his paw. That is the King of Scotland's banner. His son Zerbino is camped there. There is not a better-looking man here. Nature made him and broke the mold. Nobody shines with such virtue, grace and strength combined. Incidentally, he is Duke of Ross. The Earl of Huntley bears a gilded bar on blue for his standard. The other banner belongs to the Duke of Mark—showing the captive leopard. See, there, the insignia of many colors, with many strange birds; it is the insignia of Alcabrun the Bold, who is not duke, earl or marquis, but simply first in his own savage highlands. The Duke of Strafford's is that sign where the eagle looks directly at the sun. Earl Lurcanio, who rules in Angus, bears that bull with two greyhounds at his flanks. There you see the Duke of Albany, whose sign is the field of blue and white. The vulture tearing a green dragon stands for the Earl of Buchan. Herman, the strong lord of Forbes, has the banner of white and black. On his right hand is the lord of Errol, showing a lamp on green.

"Now look at the Irish on the plain. There are two squadrons. The Earl of Kildare leads the first; the Earl of Desmond, from the mountainous wild, leads the second. The standard of the former has a burning pine; the latter, the red band on white.

"Not just England, Scotland and Ireland are sending

men to help Charlemagne. Men have also come from Sweden and Norway, and even Iceland, and other islands naturally inimical to peace. There are sixteen thousand, give or take a few, who have come out of caves and woods, with hair all over their bodies like wild animals. They have turned the open field into a forest with their spears all around that standard which is all white. Their leader, Moray, has left the flag all white in order to paint it, later, with Moorish blood."

While Ruggiero was looking at all these fair folk prepared to save France and hearing about them from the British lord, one man after another had come to see the rare beast he rode. They all were amazed, and as the word spread, more and more came running. There was a tight circle around him by the time the lord was finished speaking. To amaze them still more, and have some fun, Ruggiero shook the reins and lightly spurred the flanks of his flying steed. It spread its wings, jumping, and flew up to the sky, leaving everyone on the spot overwhelmed with wonder. Then Ruggiero looked over England from shore to shore, and flew still farther west, toward Ireland.

And he saw fabled Ireland, where old Saint Patrick made the cave in which a man may be purged of all his sins, such is the mercy that may be found there. And he flew beyond Ireland, to another, crueller coast where, looking down, he saw Angelica chained to the naked rock.

This was the isle of tears, whose fierce, inhuman natives snatch beautiful women from every other shore to feed their monster, the Orc. She had been chained that very morning to the rock where it came every day to eat. I told you earlier how pirates seized her when they found her sleeping beside the old enchanter on the beach he had brought her to by his magic. In time, the inhospitable people of Ebuda exposed her for the beast, as naked as Nature had made her. She did not even have a veil to shade the white lily and red rose of her body— unfading in July or in December.

From high overhead, Ruggiero wondered if she were not a perfect statue of pale pink alabaster, with gold for hair, the greatest sculptor's masterpiece. But circling lower, he could see tears falling from her cheeks to her breasts, and he could see a gentle breeze stir her long, golden hair. He hovered over her, and when she looked up and he looked into her eyes, he thought of his Bradamante. Pity and love pierced him in unison and he hardly could hold back his own tears.

He had his winged steed land beside the rock, and he said, softly, "O my lady, you deserve to wear no chain but Love's. You do not deserve this, or any other evil. What perverse monster could want to fetter, and mark, those beautiful ivory hands?"

She blushed as he spoke; rose spread over the white ivory; and she would have covered herself if she had been able to move her hands. Every part of her body was beautiful, and she was modest, not shameless. But she had only tears to cover her. She hung her golden head, avoiding his eyes, and she sobbed for a moment before she could speak. Then she began, faintly, weakly, but she did not go on; her first words were drowned by a great noise from the deep water.

It was the Orc. The Orc appeared and the ocean roared. The Orc surfaced; half its immense bulk rose above tall, breaking waves, and it surged toward the shore like a tall ship driven by a rising wind.

Angelica almost fainted, half dead with terror. She was not reassured by the strange knight's kind words, for what could he do?

He spurred the rearing hippogriff and it sprang into the air over the surf. He held his lance not in the rest, but overhand, and swooping down, he struck the Orc between the eyes. And the Orc went on its way toward the rock where the savages fed it.

I do not know what that thing resembled. It was a huge, dark mass, surging like the sea itself. It looked like no other animal I know of, except for its head, with the little eyes and protruding tusks of a pig. The teeth were yellow and the inside of its mouth was like rust. The eyes were red and the skin was all dark slime. When Ruggiero struck it, the lance scraped away slime, but underneath it was like striking iron or stone.

After the first, useless blow the paladin wheeled back in air and made the second one better. The Orc did not even notice. But it did see the shadow of the hippogriff's wings skimming on the water, and it paused, and turned, and left its certain, shore-bound prey to chase the shadow. As it writhed furiously below, Ruggiero dropped to hit it again and again the way an eagle attacks a snake, not where it can bite and spit venom, but on the spine, just behind the head, where it cannot see or turn to strike back. He used his lance, he used his sword, but he could not puncture or cut its rock-hard hide.

It was like the assault of a fly against a dog. And the Orc, evidently stung a little, did at last notice; it raised its snout and snapped at the hippogriff instead of its shadow. A fly is quick. But if the dog's teeth close on it just once, the battle is over. The Orc lunged up after its tormentor again and again, meanwhile lashing the sea with its tail, raising so much spray that Ruggiero could no longer tell if the giant eagle wings still beat on air, or if his mount was swimming.

Ruggiero would have preferred a dragon ashore; he was afraid that if the spray flew so thickly much longer and soaked the feathers, both he and his steed would drown, at best. He pulled up, thinking it would be better to fight on with another weapon. He decided to dazzle the Orc with the blinding splendor enchanted in the lidded shield.

Praying that the magic would work against the immeasurable monster, he flew back to the beach. He took the ring off his finger and, in order to protect the lady from harm, he put it on hers—that selfsame ring that Bradamante took from Brunello and gave to Melissa sending it to the Indies to free Ruggiero from Alcina's clutches. Melissa, after using the ring to save him and many others then gave it to Ruggiero. Now he gave it to Angelica, partly because he was afraid it might inhibit the magic of the shield, but also because he did not want to risk hurting her eyes, which had already attracted him so much.

Angelica was too terrified to notice this; the Orc had turned and now followed where Ruggiero had flown, or merely resumed its way to its meal. It was coming more quickly. It was much closer, pushing half the sea before its belly.

Ruggiero turned again, his hippogriff rearing out of the rising water, and he tore the cover from the shield and added another sun to the sky. The light flashed in the Orc's piglike eyes, and it worked its magic as always: like a little trout in a stream some mountaineer has poisoned with lime, the Orc rolled over and lay still in the subsiding foam. Ruggiero flew to attack it again, using his spear on the exposed belly. And here the hide gave, like chain mail over soft flesh, but still he could not cut it.

Meanwhile the chained girl cried and begged him, "Come back, in God's name, sir! Free me before the Orc wakes up! Carry me away with you! Drown me in the middle of the ocean! Anything! But don't leave me here by the monster!"

So Ruggiero left the Orc alive. He flew back to the

beach and broke her fetters. He caught her up behind him, holding one helpless ivory arm around his body, and he spurred his steed. It sprang up, eager to gallop through the sky again, the knight in the saddle and the gleaming wet damsel behind. So the Orc lost a meal, one much too sweet and delicate for him. Ruggiero turned in the saddle and covered her fair eyes, cheeks and breasts with a thousand kisses, brushing away her tears with his lips.

And he abandoned his intended course. He forgot about circling Spain. He hardly noticed which way the hippogriff was flying. But as soon as he saw land appear, where Brittany juts into the ocean, he forced it to put down on the shore. This shore was heavily wooded with shady oaks, where Philomela the nightingale, seemed always to lament ancient outrage. But here the wood was broken by a meadow with a spring, and here and there a solitary mound.

Ruggiero dismounted in the meadow and made his courser fold and lower its stiff wings, but he could by no means do the same with what he had, which was stiffer. Having dismounted one steed, he could barely keep from immediately mounting another. Only his armor prevented him. He had to take off his armor first, and he tried. But he could not control his desire, and could not control his hands. With urgent, sweating fingers he trembled and fumbled at the hot, heavy plate and mail, and each time he managed to unfasten one thing he seemed to jam a couple of others. He never knew it to take so long to take off his armor.

But this chapter, my lord, is already too long. I'll put my story aside until another time, when it might yet have some interest.

ELEVEN

The Slaying of the Orc

You can control a mighty stallion with a light rein, but you cannot so easily control lust, once it is aroused and its gratification is in sight. As well expect a bear to turn away from a honeypot when he has already licked a few drops from the rim, as expect good Ruggiero to be reasonable now. What reason did he have for not having his way, taking his pleasure with the gentle Angelica, since he had her, naked, in a solitary, convenient, comfortable spot? He did not happen to think of Bradamante, and even if he had, he would have been insane not to want this girl, too; she would have moved even the severely continent Xenocrates to forget himself.

Ruggiero had thrown down his spear and his shield, and he was trying to take off his armor, when the lady modestly lowered her eyes to her beautiful nude body and noticed the ring, the precious ring that Brunello had stolen from her in Albracca. This was the ring she had carried into France when she first came from the East, with her brother, bearer of the magic lance which Astolfo picked up later. With this ring, she had nullified Malagigi's magic by Merlin's rock. With this, she had saved Orlando and others from slavery to Dragontina, in the East. With this, she had escaped, invisible, from a tower where an evil old man had held her prisoner. But why should I tell you all this? You know it all as well as I do. Brunello the dwarf had stolen it from her for King Agramante so that he could free Ruggiero. . . .

And from the moment she lost it, Fortune had scorned her and she had lost even her own country.

Now that she saw it on her hand, she was so surprised and happy that she was afraid it was a dream and did not dare believe her eyes. As in a dream, she raised the ring to her lips, and lo, it was real; she vanished from Ruggiero's sight like lightning.

Ruggiero, still struggling with his armor, looked all around, then stumbled about like a madman. He remembered the ring and was stunned with shame. He cursed his carelessness and accused the lady of ingratitude.

"Ungrateful lady!" he shouted, turning round and round, hoping she could hear him. "Is this how you repay me for what I did for you? Come back and I'll *give* you my ring! I'll give you the magic shield, too! I'll give you the flying steed! And myself! You can use me as you want! You know that. But don't hide your beautiful face like this. I know you hear me. Answer! Don't be so mean to me!"

He went groping around the spring like a blind man, grabbing the empty air, hoping to catch her, again and again.

But she was already far away, and did not pause to rest until she came to a big cave at the bottom of a hill, where she found some food, and ate. An old man who kept a herd of mares lived there, keeping the mares inside, in stalls that sheltered them at night or at midday. Angelica stayed there, unseen, the rest of that day. About vespers, refreshed, she decided to go on. She dressed herself in some rude garments, not at all her usual style. She was used to high fashion and fine colors—green, yellow, purple, azure and scarlet. But no shapeless, colorless cloth could conceal the fact that she was fair and noble. You pastoral poets may as well keep quiet about your Phyllis, Neaera, Amaryllis and the fugitive Galatea; those fair nymphs could not compare with Angelica, if I may say so. Besides rough clothing, she also picked out the best mare. And just then it occurred to her, "I might as well return to the Levant."

Ruggiero meanwhile had given up hope, at last, that she would ever reappear to him. He had stopped rushing about after her, and he had stopped calling her, too. He went to where he had left his steed, in order to remount and fly on, and he found that it had loosed its reins from the branch where he had tied it, or thought he had tied it, and it too had disappeared. Wherever it had flown, it was already too far away to be seen.

His losses crushed him, but he was troubled most by the loss of the precious ring, precious to him not so much for its magic powers as because his lady had sent it to him. Ashamed and grieved, he took up his arms and his armor again, and trudged away from the sea, up the grassy slope to the mouth of a wide, wooded valley, where he chose the widest path he could see and entered the deep, dark forest.

He had not gone far before he heard, on his right where the trees grew most thickly, a sudden noise: the dreadful clash of arms.

He hurried through the trees in that direction and soon came upon a great battle being fought in a narrow space between two who seemed bent on avenging unmentionable crimes, they fought so relentlessly: a savage giant and a knight in armor. The knight was on the defensive, using shield more than sword, leaping about, dodging, while the giant held a heavy mace in both hands and swung it against him again and again. The knight's horse already lay dead in the path, its skull crushed.

Ruggiero stood and watched the fight. He hoped the

knight would win, but not knowing the cause, he did not want to interfere.

Of a sudden, the giant struck the knight on the helmet, a heavy blow, and the knight fell and lay still. And then the giant bent over, holding the mace ready to hit again in one hand, and unlacing the knight's helmet with the other, so that Ruggiero could for the first time see the knight's face.

And the face he saw was Bradamante's!

The giant raised his mace and Ruggiero shouted his challenge, already advancing with naked sword. But the giant did not wait for a second fight. He snatched up the unconscious girl and threw her over his shoulder and ran off like a wolf with a lamb, an eagle with a dove.

Now that Ruggiero saw how much his help was needed, he went running after as fast as he could; but the giant led the way with such long, swift strides that Ruggiero could barely keep him in sight, much less help his lady. So the one ran and the other followed, down the overshadowed gloomy path which went on, always widening, until it opened on a great meadow in the forest.

So much for Ruggiero, for the moment. I have to get back to Orlando, who had thrown King Cimosco's thunderer into the deep sea so that it might never be found again. Much good that did us! Our cruel Enemy, who invented it to do us almost as much harm as when he tempted Eve with the forbidden fruit, had a magician find it again in our grandfathers' time, or a little before. Though it had remained hidden a hundred fathoms down for so many years, he brought it to the surface by magic and sold it to the Germans. They worked on it, the Devil working on their minds, until they learned how to use it. Soon after that, Italy and France and all the other countries learned the cruel art. Some cast bronze tubes; others bored iron ones. Some made the barrels wide, and some made them narrow. Whatever the makers are pleased to call them—mortars, guns, simple and double cannon, falcon, saker, culverine— all of them shatter steel and pulverize stone, opening a way wherever they are fired.

Poor soldier, bring all your arms and armor back to the forge, even your sword. Have everything melted down again. Just put a musket on your shoulder. That's all that matters now.

O damned invention, how did you ever win a place in man's heart? Through you, all martial glory is destroyed. Through you, the profession of arms has lost all honor. Through you, valor and virtue are vanquished. The brave do not prove themselves now; the weakest often get the best of a fight. Damned machine! Through you, so many lords and knights are to be overthrown and buried before the end of this present war, which all the world, but mostly Italy, mourns, that it would not be too much for me to declare that the most malign geniuses who ever existed were those who first imagined such abominable machines. And I believe that God, to avenge this eternally, will send their souls to the very bottom of the abyss, next to Judas.

But I forget myself; we are following the knight who longs to reach the island of Ebuda, where fair and delicate women are fed to a sea monster.

The wind did not cooperate. It blew from right or left or from behind, always so faintly that the ship could made little headway, and sometimes it did not blow at all, or it blew against him, and then it was so strong that the ship was forced to turn back for a time. So God willed that he did not get there before the King of Ireland, and Ebuda itself presented no problem for him, as I will tell you in a couple of pages.

When Orlando did reach the island, he told his pilot, "Anchor here, and give me the boat, because I don't want any company when I land. And I want your biggest anchor, with your biggest cable, to take with me. You'll see why if I run into the monster."

So he set out in the skiff, the ship's anchor all but sinking it, the cable all but filling it. He left all his armor and his weapons aboard the ship, except his sword, and all alone he turned the skiff to the rocky, empty shore and drew both oars to his chest, making progress crabwise toward the rocks at his back. It was the time of day when fair, loving Aurora spreads her yellow locks before the red sun, half-risen, half-hidden still—not without arousing the usual indignation of her husband, immortal but withered Tithonis, who had reason to be jealous. And it was clear and very calm.

A good stone's throw from the rocky beach, Orlando thought he heard a weak, low sob. He turned to his left and looked carefully along the shore, and in the dawning light he saw a woman, naked as when she was born, tied to a rock with the water at her feet. Because he was still pretty far out, and because she kept her head down, he could not tell who she was. He pulled on the oars and sped nearer, turning again for a closer look.

But just at that moment, he heard the waters roar and the rocks echo all around. Looking back, he saw the monster almost obliterating the sea under its belly at its first surge into the upper air. You have seen heavy clouds, dark with rain, rushing up a valley, filling it with night, or rather, a darkness worse than night, extinguishing the daylight from mountain wall to mountain wall. The beast's approach was like that. Waves so great they tossed the skiff high in the air raced before the monster. Orlando watched its coming calmly. His face did not change expression and his heart did not skip a beat. In order to shield the woman and attack the monster as soon as possible, he rowed directly between her and the Orc. Then, having planned everything he would do, he moved quickly and surely. He left his sword in its sheath. Instead, he took up the anchor. Then he calmly waited.

As soon as the Orc was near and saw Orlando in the boat, it opened its mouth to swallow him. Open, its mouth was big enough for a man on horseback to ride inside without ducking. The skiff moved toward that open mouth as if it were in a swift mountain stream, with rapids ahead, and there were the teeth, to catch and splinter it. But Orlando stood up and jumped. The teeth never closed on the boat because by that time Orlando had fixed the anchor in the palate and the soft squirming tongue and the Orc could not close its mouth.

Orlando was like a miner who props up the earth wherever he digs so that it will not bury him, suddenly, at his work. And that anchor was so wide that Orlando himself could not reach the distance from hook to hook.

And as soon as Orlando was certain that the anchor was secure and the Orc could not close its hideous jaws, he drew his sword and began slashing the rusty walls of the dark cave of its mouth. The Orc was no more capable of defending itself from the knight in its throat than is a fortress after the enemy has taken its stronghold. Overcome by surprise and pain, it writhed on the surface. But there was one thing it could still do: it dived to the bottom in its frenzy, and writhed there. Now water rushed down its open throat and almost carried Orlando into the very belly of the monster. But he clung to the anchor and cut and thrust as long as he was able to hold his breath.

By that time the mad beast was vomiting water, blood and slime, and Orlando kicked off from the anchor in its gorge and swam up to the surface, never letting go of the cable he had tied to the anchor.

He surfaced and swam as fast as he could to the shore, where he set his feet against the rock and pulled the cable in. The Orc, with the anchor caught in its mouth, was forced to follow. Orlando could exert more force in one tug on that cable than a capstan could in ten turns. Like a wild bull that suddenly feels a lasso catch one horn, and leaps and turns about and raises and lowers its head, unable to free itself, so the Orc was drawn writhing and wriggling helplessly by the force of Orlando's arm. It followed where he pulled and it could not escape.

All this time, blood was pouring out of its mouth in a great stream, and its tail was lashing so that you could see bottom in the cove. Red spray dyed the shores and rose to dim the light of the morning sun. To this day, that place might be called another Red Sea. And the echoing sounds of the sea and of the Orc itself were indescribable.

Old Proteus must have come out of his grotto when he heard the Orc begin its uproar. Seeing Orlando escape the Orc, and drag it after him to the shore, that god must have forgotten his herds and abandoned Ebuda, to flee through the deep ocean. And the tumult grew so loud that Neptune himself hitched his dolphins to his chariot and went back to Ethiopia, or somewhere else as far away, in a hurry. Ino, with her son Melicertes crying on her shoulder, and the Oceanides with their disheveled hair, and Glauci and Tritons and all the other spirits of the sea scattered in all directions to save themselves.

Orlando pulled the horrendous creature ashore, and once it was there he did not have to trouble himself any more about it; it was dead by that time.

But many of the islanders had come running to watch

the strange battle, and in their vain religion they thought Orlando's holy work was profane. They said it was most provocative. They said it would make Proteus their enemy again, and he would send his sea beasts to land again, renewing the ancient war. They concluded that they had better sue the offended god for peace before that happened. And they assumed that the first thing to do was throw the hero into the water and drown him. The idea spread among them like wildfire. They went down to the beach with slings, arrows, spears and swords, and attacked him from all sides.

Orlando was amazed by their ingratitude. He had expected thanks for killing the monster, not insults. But he was no more afraid of the mob than a bear, led through a fair by some Russian or Lithuanian, is afraid of the barking of the little dogs, if he even notices them. He could disperse them with a single blow.

They crowded round Orlando with all their weapons, and he drew Durindana and made room. They had not expected any trouble, since he wore no armor and did not even carry a shield. They had not known that his skin was harder than diamond, from head to foot, but they found out. They could not touch him. They could not defend themselves against him, either. He killed thirty and maybe a few more with ten blows. That cleared the whole area, and he was on his way to free the woman when a new tumult came to his ears.

While he had been occupied in this cove, the Irish had landed on another shore, without opposition. Pitilessly, they were slaughtering all the people they found, with no regard for age, sex or condition, they were so outraged by the human sacrifices of Ebuda. The Irish met little resistance partly because the islanders were taken by surprise, partly because there were not very many of them anyway, and those few had no leaders with them. They were used to attacking others. They never had been attacked like this. Their property was sacked, their houses were set afire, their walls were razed and they were all killed; not a single one was left alive.

What Orlando heard was this strife and ruin. He paid no attention. He went on to the woman tied naked to the rock for the Orc to devour. He thought he knew her. The closer he came, the surer he was: Olimpia, who had gained so evil a reward for her faithfulness, poor Olimpia, whom Love had scorned and Fortune delivered into the hands of the pirates of Ebuda on one and the same day.

She recognized him when he came near, but she kept her head down and not only did not speak, but did not dare raise her eyes to his face, because she was naked. To put her more at ease, Orlando asked what bad luck had brought her to Ebuda, considering he had left her and her consort so happy together.

"I do not know if I ought to thank you for saving me from this death," she said, "or complain that on account of you my misery has been prolonged. Oh, I must thank you. That kind of death would have been too terrible. But only death can help me, and I would thank you more if you would slay me now."

Then, crying, she went on to tell how her husband had betrayed her, leaving her asleep on the desert island where the pirates had found her. While she spoke, she turned modestly, the way artists portray Diana, hiding her breasts and her belly from Acteon as much as she can, and revealing only her beautiful back and buttocks. Orlando, having unchained her, tried to signal his ship in order to get something for her to wear.

At this point, Oberto came upon them, Oberto, King of Ireland, who had heard that the sea monster was stretched out on the shore, and even that a knight had gone swimming, caught it with an anchor, and pulled it in like a fisherman, or more like those who pull great ships against the current of some river, except that he had done it all alone. Ebuda being subdued, Oberto left his men to destroy what little was left, and went to see if there was any truth in the story. He knew Orlando, though the knight was covered with blood and filth from the Orc. He had known it would be Orlando, if the story were true. He had been a page in France, until he left to accept the crown when his father died, the year before, so he would know Orlando anywhere. He ran to greet and embrace him, taking off his helmet.

Orlando was no less happy to see the king, and after they had greeted each other enthusiastically, Orlando told Oberto how the girl had been betrayed, and by whom, by Bireno, the man who least ought to have harmed her in any way. He told the Irish king how she had proved her love for Bireno, losing her family and her wealth, and at last willing to lose her life for him.

While he talked, Olimpia was weeping. Her fair face was like a spring day, with the rain falling while the sun is shining; and like the nightingale singing sweetly amidst the green boughs, Love seemed to bathe his wings in her fair tears while joying in the clear light of her eyes. Love fired his arrows in that sweet light. He quenched them in the streams that flowed over the red and white flowers of her skin. Then he shot the Irish youth who was defended by neither shield nor double mail and leather. The King of Ireland stood and looked at her and felt wounded in the heart and did not know why.

Olimpia's beauties were very rare—not only her hair, face and throat, but everything ordinarily covered. The whiteness of her breasts surpassed that of untouched snow, and they were smoother than ivory to the touch. They were high, and the valley between was

deep, shadowed but smooth as if just filled with snow.
Her flat belly, broad hips and perfect thighs might
have been carved and polished by Phidias, or some
even more skilled sculptor. If she had appeared to the
Phrygian shepherd, Paris, in the valley of Ida, I do
not know that Venus would have won the golden apple,
though she beat the other goddesses; and Paris would
not have gone to Laconia, to violate sacred hospitality,
but would have said, "Stay with Menelaus, Helen; I
do not want any other but her." And if she were in
Crotona when Zeuxis planned to make his imaginary
portrait of Helen, one worthy to stand in the temple of
Juno, he would not have had to collect so many nude
models, to take one feature from one, another from
another; he would not have needed any model but
Olimpia, because all beauties were in her. I do not
believe that Bireno ever saw her naked, or he never
could have been so cruel as to leave her on the desert
island.

Oberto could not hide the fire he took from her. He
tried to comfort her, giving her hope that her present
bad fortune would turn to good. He promised to go
back to Holland with her and restore her kingdom and
avenge her wrong on the liar, the traitor, Bireno. He
vowed to use all the power that Ireland could afford,
and he vowed to do it immediately. Meanwhile, he had
a search made for gowns not burned or bloody. There
was no need to search far. His looters had found
a vast store of varied clothing taken from those women
who had been fed to the hungry monster, every day,
for so long. Although some of these gowns were very
old, others were fresh and new. The very best were
brought down to the shore. Oberto regretted not being
able to clothe her as well as he would have liked, but
that was because nothing seemed fit to decorate so
beautiful a body. The Florentines never wove silk so

fair nor gold so fine. No human being could expend the time and skill it would take. Even the clothing of gods would not have satisfied him, having seen her naked body.

Orlando was happy to see Oberto's love for her, for a number of reasons. For one, Bireno had to be punished, but he did not care to do it himself, because he had come to help not Olimpia but his own lady, if she was there. It was soon clear that she was not. Whether she ever had been, however, he did not know. Everyone who had lived on the island was dead. No one was left to tell him if she had been there.

The next day, they all sailed away together. Orlando's ship accompanied the others to Ireland, because it was on his way to France. But he rested there less than one full day. They could not persuade him to stay any longer. Love, who sent him after his lady, would not let him rest. Before setting sail again, he had Oberto vow to protect and maintain Olimpia. He did not have to ask, since Oberto meant to do much more for her than keep that promise, but he wanted to be sure he was free. Only a few days later, Oberto gathered his men and then, in league with the kings of England and Scotland, he liberated Holland, took Frisia too, turned Bireno's own Zeeland to rebellion against him and did not end the war until he had killed the betrayer—not that such punishment was enough. Oberto made Olimpia, who had been countess, a great queen.

But back to the paladin Orlando, who spread his sails and traveled night and day until he furled them again in the same port he had left long ago. There he armed himself and jumped on his Brigliadoro and left the winds and waves behind.

I believe that he did many things worthy of eternal song during the rest of that winter. But he did them secretly. Orlando was always readier to do good deeds than report them, so many of them were never publicized, unless there happened to be witnesses. He passed the rest of that winter so quietly that as far as the world was concerned, nothing was known. But when the sun rose in Aries, the good, golden ram, and Zephyrus turned soft and light, bringing sweet spring back to France, news of Orlando's marvelous deeds came forth with the flowers and grass.

From plain to hill, from meadowland to shore, he rode on, full of pain and woe, when, on entering a forest, a long scream of fear and sorrow wounded his ears. He spurred his horse and drew his sword and hurried in its direction. I'll tell you what he found next time, if you are willing to bear with me.

TWELVE

The Palace of Illusions

When Ceres, after visiting the mother-goddess Cybele, on Ida, came back to that lonely valley by Etna where Jupiter buried the giant Enceladus, and did not find her own dear daughter, Proserpina, where she had left her—for Pluto had taken her away—the goddess tore her hair, her cheeks, her breasts, and at last pulled up two pine trees, ignited them in Vulcan's fire, making them magically unextinguishable, and then, holding one in each hand, mounted her dragon chariot and flew circling to search the woods, the fields, the hills, the plains, the valleys, the streams and lakes, all the land and all the sea. And after she had searched the whole upper world, she went down to Tartarus, below.

If Orlando's power had equaled his will, he would have looked for Angelica as thoroughly as the Eleusian goddess looked for Proserpina; he would have toured all of Earth and Heaven and the depths of Hell. Not having the chariot nor the dragons to pull it, he still looked as best he could. He covered France, and he was ready to ride through Italy and Germany, through New and Old Castile, and then to cross the sea to Libya.

And while he was thinking of all the lands he might search, he heard that scream, spurred on, and saw a knight trotting ahead of him on a large destrier. He held a sorrowing damsel on his saddlebow. Crying and struggling, she called back for help from the prince of

179

Anglante, and to Orlando she seemed to be his beloved Angelica.

Seeing his lady and goddess being so miserably carried off, Orlando exploded in wrath, and called after the knight in a horrendous voice, called and challenged him, and drove Brigliadoro on at full speed. The knight did not stop or answer or even look back; he hung on to his noble prey, his great prize, and galloped recklessly through the trees so fast that the wind would have had trouble catching him. Orlando rode as recklessly after him. The forest was filled with the damsel's screams and the sound of thudding hoofs and cracking branches. Riding madly like this, they suddenly emerged into a wide meadow, in the middle of which stood a big palace, rich with fine work in diverse marbles.

The knight rode even faster over the open space and right through the gilded gate, with the lady in his arms.

Brigliadoro got there not long after with the fierce Orlando, who looked all around as soon as he was inside but did not see either the evil knight or his victim or his horse. Orlando quickly dismounted, raging, and went where Brigliadoro could not carry him. He ran here and there and did not pause until he had been down each corridor and looked into every room. When he had searched the whole ground floor in vain, he ran up the stairs and spent as much time and effort on the second floor—as vainly. He saw beds decorated with silk and gold, floors all covered with carpeting, walls entirely hidden by tapestries and curtains. He saw nothing of Angelica or the enemy. He went through the whole palace, then went back and started again.

And while Count Orlando went back and forth, up and down, full of worry, he met other knights—

Ferrau, Brandimarte, King Gradasso, King Sacripante and others, all looking high and low as he was, and all complaining bitterly about the invisible lord of the wicked palace, all blaming him for some loss—the theft of a destrier, or a lady, or something or someone else. He did not recognize any of the other searchers, however, on account of magic there. And all of them stayed, and did not leave their cage, though the gates always stood open. Many of them had stayed in that trap for weeks or months, and none had ever left.

Orlando, after searching the strange place four or five times, said to himself, "I could spend the rest of my life like this, and the thief could have taken her out through another exit, and by now they could be far away." Thinking this, he went out into the green field that surrounded the palace.

While he circled the building, keeping his eyes on the ground for any indication of a new trail, he heard a call from a window and looked up. He thought he heard that divine voice, thought he saw that divine face: Angelica, who had divided him from himself. She seemed to be weeping, begging, "Help! Help! For my virginity more than my life and soul! Oh, am I going to be raped by this thief? And in the presence of my Orlando? Oh, Orlando, kill me before you let him rape me!"

He ran back inside and found the room, but she was not there. Then he searched the whole palace as thoroughly and as furiously as before, overtired and in pain tempered by high hope.

This happened time and again, and he never found her. Sometimes he stopped, and then he heard the voice like Angelica's, begging for help. And if he were in one place, it came from another, upstairs or down, and he could not tell where.

Now to return to Ruggiero. I left him following a giant who was carrying a lady who seemed to be Bradamante, out of the woods, over a wide field. You will recognize the place. He came where Orlando had come before him. The giant ran through the gate. Ruggiero followed, into the courtyard, looking round the galleries, but he did not see the giant or the lady anywhere. He could not imagine how they could have disappeared so quickly. He looked for them, back and forth, time after time, and never found her. He went through rooms, galleries and halls, upstairs and down, and in the space beneath the stairs. He thought they might be out in the meadow, or in the surrounding woods, and he went outside. A voice called him, as a voice had called Orlando—and the others. And he also went back.

It was only one voice, only one person. To Orlando, it appeared as Angelica, to Ruggiero as Bradamante of Dordona, but it was neither. And when it appeared to Gradasso, or any of the other knights who wandered in that place, it seemed to be whomever, or whatever, that knight wanted most, and had lost, and was looking for.

All this was a rare, new spell that Atlante of Carena had devised, in order to keep Ruggiero so busy that the evil influence he feared might not fall upon him from the stars—and he would not meet an early death. Atlante's own castle had not held Ruggiero in Africa, and the illusory fortress of iron had not held him, and Alcina had not held him on her island, but now Atlante plotted again.

And he trapped not only Ruggiero, but all those others, the most famous knights in France, so that Ruggiero would not die by their hands. For none of the victims recognized each other; Atlante saw to that by feeding them magic.

As for Angelica, the true Angelica, not the simulation Orlando was looking for in Atlante's palace, she had not been raped. She was still safe, wearing her own anti-magic ring. Invisible, Angelica had found some food, clothing and a mare at the mountain cave, and now she intended to return to her own fair land, Cathay. Orlando or Sacripante would have accompanied her, and she would have accepted either one as readily, for his company, if not for his love. She had no intention of taking either of them as a lover. But the trip was so long, she thought she could use a trustworthy guide and protector.

She searched now for Orlando, now for Sacripante, in towns, villages, woods and fields. It was a long time before she found any sign of either one of them. Then luck at last brought her to the place where Atlante had snared both of them, along with Ferrau, Gradasso and all the others.

Safe from magic herself, and invisible even to Atlante, she came to the meadow. There was no garden or palace. Instead, she saw many armed knights and a few ladies wandering around and around a great dead tree that lay uprooted in the middle of the meadow. She saw all their steeds tied to the roots of the tree, feeding peacefully or drinking from a pool where the tree had grown. She saw old Atlante crouching there, watching Ruggiero.

Avoiding him, she loosened the ring on her finger, caught glimpses of his illusions and understood his trap. She saw Orlando, Sacripante and the others, and she could not make up her mind. Orlando was the strongest, but she thought about it and began to wonder if she could send him back so easily, once he had taken her home. Sacripante would be easier to handle, she thought, so at last she chose him.

Seeing him coming, she walked ahead of him until

a moment when the others were out of sight. Then she kissed the ring and appeared. He immediately caught her in his arms. Before she had explained they must escape, both Orlando and Ferrau came upon them. She slipped out of Sacripante's arms, mounted her mare and fled across the meadow. All three had been close enough to Angelica and that ring; not only had she appeared, but all magic was dispelled for them for the moment. They took their horses and raced after her.

Atlante saw them go. He could not stop them, because of the spell of her beauty. He did not even try. But no others escaped, and Atlante did not mind losing these three, since he had Ruggiero.

Orlando and Sacripante were fully armed. They had not dared put off their armor while looking through the palace for their goddess, Angelica. It was no more a burden for knights like them to wear all their armor than it is for us to wear ordinary clothes, anyway. The third man, Ferrau, had all his armor except a helmet. He would not wear one until he had taken Orlando's. As you may recall, he had sworn this to Argalia's ghost in the stream. But even without a helmet, no one in that Palace of Illusions had recognized him, of course.

Angelica rode madly away because she did not care to meet all three lovers together. She led them into the woods, some distance from the false palace, where she no longer feared the evil magician's power against them. Then she kissed the ring that had saved her from so much discomfort so often. Again she disappeared, leaving them bewildered. And now that she had both of them and Ferrau as well, she changed her mind about getting either one of them to guide her back home. She decided the ring alone would have to do.

The knights slowed down and looked about blankly, like hounds baffled in the chase by a clever hare or fox. Angelica laughed and watched their progress. There was only one path in these woods. They assumed that she had continued riding down it, ahead of them, and they hurried on. Angelica kept a tighter rein, and when they had passed she followed at leisure. Meanwhile, they came to a place where the path disappeared, and they began examining the grass for prints.

Ferrau, always proudest of the proud, pushed ahead of the other two, then turned, gave them a dirty look, and yelled, "Where are you going? Don't follow me! Turn back, or choose another way, if you don't want to die. Neither in loving my lady, nor in chasing her, do I believe in putting up with company."

Orlando said to Sacripante, "What more could he say if he took us for whores?" Then he looked at Ferrau and said quietly, "You pig, if you were wearing a helmet, I'd teach you some manners."

"I don't care whether I have a helmet on," said the Spaniard. "Why should you? I can back up whatever I say without a helmet, against both of you."

Turning to the King of Circassia, Orlando said, "Please lend him your helmet, until I've treated his madness. I've never heard anything like it."

"Who, indeed, could be crazier?" the king answered. "But if you really think that's a fair request, lend him your own helmet, for me. Let me assure you, I am no less capable of punishing a madman than you are."

"You fools!" Ferrau shouted. "As if I couldn't get a helmet to wear if I wanted one! If I wanted one, I'd have both of yours by now, like it or not. I don't need a helmet! The reason I've gone without one is only a vow, and I will go without one until I have that fine one Orlando the French paladin wears on his head."

"Then," said the count, smiling, "you think you are good enough with your head uncovered to do to Orlando what he did to the son of Agolante, in Aspramont? I think that if you faced him, you'd just shiver from head to toe, forget about the helmet and quietly give him all your own armor, and your weapons, too."

But the bragging Spaniard scoffed, "I've already pressed Orlando so hard, so many times, that I could have taken his armor easily, all of it, not just his helmet. And if I didn't, it's because it didn't occur to me at the time. I didn't want to. Now I do, and I expect to do it easily next time."

Orlando lost his patience and yelled, "Liar, foul Marrano, in what country, and when, did you ever beat me in combat? I am the paladin you're bragging about! You think I'm far away, but here I am. Now see if you can take my helmet. See if you can dent it! Or see if I'm not good enough to take all the rest of your armor. And I don't want any advantage over you."

With that, he doffed his own helmet and hung it on the branch of a beech tree, and at almost the same moment he drew Durindana.

Ferrau was not afraid, though he was surprised. He drew his own sword and got ready, his shield high to cover his naked head.

So the two warriors, their horses circling each other, began to feint and probe, trying each other with steel where their armor was joined and where it was thinnest. There was not a better match in the world; these two knights were almost equal in both strength and ardor, and neither one of them could be wounded.

I suppose you have heard before, my lord, that Ferrau was charmed all over, except in the navel, where he took nourishment in the womb, and until the day he died he kept that dubious spot always armored in seven well-tempered plates of steel. The prince of

Anglante was equally enchanted, except on the soles of his feet, but he was quite capable of protecting them. Otherwise, both men were harder than diamond, if we may rely on history here. Apparently both went on their quests in armor more for show than from necessity.

So their fight became a fearful thing to see. Ferrau, stabbing or hacking, did not miss a blow. And at each stroke of Orlando's, his opponent's plate and mail came apart, broke open, shattered.

Invisible, Angelica was the only one watching, the sole witness to this terrifying spectacle. For the King of Circassia, still believing that she had ridden on, and seeing Ferrau and Orlando busy, rode on himself. Only Angelica looked on, no longer laughing. The fight grew so hard and dreadful, with no prospect of ending soon, that she decided to break it up. Rather than appear, which might be too dangerous, she thought of taking the helmet they were fighting over and see what they would do when it was gone. Not that she intended to keep it. She fully intended to give it back to the count.

Taking it down, she held it in her lap and watched a little longer, then rode away without speaking to the battling knights. She was afraid to call any attention to herself. She simply went the way Sacripante had gone. The sound of their combat hid the sound of her mare's hoofs.

They were so angry and intent that they did not notice anything for a while. Then Ferrau spared a glance for the prize and pulled back, saying, "He's treated us like a couple of fools! Where is it? He's stolen it! The beautiful helmet!"

Orlando also drew back, turned to look, saw it was gone and blazed with even hotter anger, also assuming that the third knight had taken it away. He pulled hard on the reins, turning Brigliadoro, and spurred and went after him with Ferrau close behind. They followed the trail through the forest, paused for only a moment where two tracks diverged, and then the count was riding to the left, into a valley, where the Circassian had in fact gone. Ferrau went the other way, still on the hillside, on the trail that was Angelica's.

Meanwhile, Angelica had come to a pleasant, inviting spot, with a cool spring in the shade. Still invisible, and not expecting pursuit, she hung the helmet on a little bough without tying it there. Then she dismounted and tied the mare to a sapling, where it could reach the rich grass beside the water.

The Spanish knight heard her, though he did not see her. Dismounting, he crept up on her. He saw her mare, since it was visible again. He also saw the helmet. She heard his exclamation and saw him go for it, calling for his own horse to follow. She ran to her mare, which disappeared from others' view at her touch. Mounting it, she rode for the helmet, but Ferrau had already knocked it down. He felt her horse ride by him, invisibly. He heard its hoofs, and its passing on the grass, then through the bushes, as she went on, to get away from him. He forgot about the helmet.

Remounting cost him little time, but it was enough. She fled like a breeze. He followed hoofbeats and the rustling of the foliage. But he never came near enough to touch her. At last, she reached open ground under high, old pine trees, and there he had to give up the chase.

Cursing Mohammed and Termagant and all the priests and scribes of his Law, Ferrau returned to the spring where the count's helmet still lay on the grass. He picked it up and put it on. There was no doubt whatever about its identity, because letters had been incised along the edge, telling where Orlando had earned it, how and when and from whom. So the pagan rearmed head and neck at last, according to his vow.

After he had tied this good helmet on, he reminded himself that to be fully satisfied, he still ought to find Angelica, who appeared and disappeared like lightning, nightmare, succubus or ghost. He went after her again, but he found no trace of her. When he finally lost all hope, he returned to the Spanish camp by Paris, trying to mitigate his frustrated lust by thinking only of the helmet which he now wore comfortably, just as he had sworn he would.

When Orlando heard about this, he looked for Ferrau. It took him a long time to find him. He did not get that helmet off Ferrau's head until that day on the bridge when, as other books tell, he finally killed him.

Angelica went on her way after escaping from Ferrau, but she did not travel so happily, because she was sorry about the helmet.

"I interfered, and took it and lost it," she told herself. "Of course I could not have given him what he wanted. But I didn't have to take his helmet. He really deserved better than that, after all he did for me. I took it with good intentions, God knows, but it didn't turn out as I intended. I only wanted to stop that fight. I didn't want that brutal Spaniard to get what he wanted, on account of me."

So she went on, blaming herself, but with no other real thought than of returning to the Orient. Most of the time she went invisibly, but sometimes she revealed herself to people, when it was convenient. After crossing much of the country, she arrived in a wood where she found a youth lying between two dead companions with a bad wound in his chest.

But I'll say no more about Angelica right now, because I have to tell you a lot of other things first. And I turn, not to Ferrau or Sacripante, but to Orlando. He demands that before I do anything else, I recount the labor and affliction he endured in his great desire for what, at last, he never got.

At the first city he came to, he put on a new helmet, because he did not want to be recognized. He took the first one he could get. He did not even look to see if it was well-tempered or not. Good or bad, it made little difference to him, since he was so certain of his enchanted invulnerability. With his head covered, anyway, he continued his quest, by day, by night, in rain and sun; nothing hindered him.

It was in the hour when Phoebus drives his dew-coated horses out of the sea, and Aurora goes scattering red and yellow flowers of light all about the sky, and the stars were leaving their dance, already putting on their veils, when, near Paris one day, Orlando was called upon to prove himself again. He encountered two squadrons of Saracens. One was led by Manilardo, the old King of Norizia, who had once been fierce and brave, but by now was fitter for advice than help. Alzirdo, King of Tremison, considered perfect among the African knights, led the other.

With the other pagan forces, these had wintered near the city, in all the surrounding villages and towns. King Agramante had wasted more than one day attempting to wipe out Paris by storm. Now he wanted to lay closer siege, since he could not take the city otherwise. To do this, he had an infinite host; besides those who had come with him, and those Spaniards who had followed the royal banner of Marsilio, he had bought many Frenchmen, too; for he had subjugated everything from Paris to the river of Arles, and all of Gascony except some of its fortresses.

Now all the brooks were beginning to loosen and release their cold ice in warmer water. The fields were beginning to sprout new grass. The bushes and trees were renewing their foliage with fresh, tender buds and leaves. And King Agramante was assembling all those who had followed him into France, and all the others, to review his entire army and get his affairs in better shape. For this reason, the kings of Tremison and Norizia were riding to the mustering of the entire host. And Orlando, as I said, happened to meet them in his search for the woman who kept his heart locked in a prison of love.

As Alzirdo approached and saw the count, who had his visor up, he was amazed by his look and his bearing, his glance fierce and manifest with wrath, his bearing so proud that the god of war seemed second to him. Alzirdo correctly judged him a warrior of great prowess, but unfortunately he wanted to test him. Alzirdo was young and arrogant and prized for his courage and his strength. He spurred his horse to joust with Orlando immediately. It would have been better for him if he had stayed at the head of his file; in the encounter, the prince of Anglante made him fall pierced through the heart. His horse bolted in fear because there was no one to hold the reins. And as the youth was falling, with his blood gushing out from the largest vein, a sudden and horrendous shout filled the air; raging, the pagans came at the count in disorder, ready to stab and hack him to pieces, while others deluged him with arrows.

Wild pigs sound like that, as they run from the hills or the fields if the wolf comes out of a hidden den or a bear comes down the mountain and takes one of them; they grunt and squeal their protest. Protesting thus, the barbarous mob moved in on the count, yelling, "Get him! Get him!"

His breastplate and his shield took thousands of lances, arrows and swords at one and the same time. One pagan struck him on the back with a mace, too. Others jabbed spears at his sides. But Orlando was never afraid, and he thought no more of the vile crowd and their weapons than the wolf thinks of the sheep in the flock. He had in his hand that lightning sword that had already put so many other Saracens to death—and anyone who wanted to keep track of how many fell here would have a hard time. No sooner had they closed on him than the road was running red with blood. A moment, and it was scarcely wide enough to hold the corpses. They soon rose around him in a single, circular wall. No buckler, helmet, cotton-padded vest, no strips of cloth wound about the head in thousands of turns could fend off the fatal Durindana, wherever it came down. Groans and screams pierced the air, and so did flying arms and hands and severed heads.

Around and around the little field, cruel Death circled in many different—but all horrible—guises; and Death said to himself, "In Orlando's hand, Durindana is better than a hundred of my scythes."

One blow hardly waited for the other, and soon enough all that remained began to flee, though they had hurried to him, expecting to overwhelm him because he was alone. Now there was none who looked for his friends to go with him, much less to help a friend out of that trouble. They ran and rode on every side, none even asking directions.

Valor circled, like Death, holding up the mirror that shows every wrinkle of the soul itself. Not one of the Saracens would look into it except one very old man, infirm on account of age but not weakened in spirit. That man saw how much better death would be than dishonor in flight, after their dishonorable attack. It

was the King of Norizia alone who stood and set his
lance and rode again at the knight of France, and
broke the point on the upper edge of the shield held
by that paladin whom nothing moves. Durindana was
ready and hit King Manilardo in passing. Fortune
helped the old man then. The hard steel turned as it fell,
because full strokes with the edge are not always easy in
such circumstances. But the blow still made him tumble
out of his saddle, stunned.

Orlando did not turn to take notice; he went on
smashing, cleaving, chopping, slaughtering the others.
To all of them, it seemed that he was at their backs.
Like starlings before the hawk, both squadrons flew—
those who had not fallen. The bloody sword did not
slow down and stop before the road and the wood
seemed empty of living men before Orlando.

They had got in his way. Now the way was clear.
But he had some doubt about which way he was
going, though he knew all that country very well. He
just went on at random, his thoughts always far ahead
of him, and always afraid that he was taking the
wrong road. So he turned, and turned again, but always went on, asking for her as often as possible,
never hearing a word about her. As if beside himself,
he began to ignore roads anyway; he just went on
through fields and woods.

In the woods at night, he happened to come to the
foot of a mountain where he saw a light. It came from
a cleft rock far ahead of him, and it looked like wings
waving in the dark. Orlando approached to see if
Angelica were hidden there. Men who hunt the timid
hare and lose track of her have to go and look under
each thicket, each thornbush and lowly juniper and
even in the stubble of the open fields; thus Orlando
searched for his lady with great care, wherever hope
happened to lead him. He hurried toward that ray of

light and reached its source, a narrow vent in the mountainside, just broad enough to pass through. The cave or caves inside were screened by saplings and thornbushes which made a protecting wall for whomever lived there. By day, the place would not be seen at all. With a little care, the light would not have revealed it in the dark, either. Orlando guessed what kind of place it was, but wanted to make sure.

After tying Brigliadoro outside, he quietly went in, as quietly as he could, through the thick branches; he did not call for anyone to admit him. Inside, he descended, step by step, into a tomb where people were buried alive. The cave was not small. It had been chiseled out to make a wide vault. Although the entrance did not let much light in, the cavern was not entirely without daylight down below, because a window had been cut in the rock.

In the middle of the cave, a good-looking girl was sitting beside the fire. She must have been little past fifteen years old, as far as the count could tell at first glance. And she was so beautiful that she made the savage place look like a paradise, though her eyes were full of tears. There was an old woman there, too, back in the shadows. The two of them were quarreling, as women so often do, but as the count came down the stairs they both shut up.

Orlando greeted them with the courtesy we always owe women, and they got up to welcome him as courteously, allowing for their surprise at his intrusion and their alarm at his fierce looks.

Then Orlando asked the damsel who could be so discourteous, unjust, barbarous and atrocious as to keep so gentle and lovely a girl buried in that cave. She had trouble answering him. At first, passionate sobbing interrupted her, distorting her coral lips, showing teeth like precious pearls. Her tears streamed down over the lily and rose of her cheeks, and she had to swallow some.

Please listen to the rest in the next chapter, lord, because it is time to finish this one.

THIRTEEN

The Prophecy of Melissa

The knights in those days were very lucky, because in hidden valleys, wild forests and dark caves, in the dens of serpents, bears and lions, they were always finding what good judges rarely find nowadays in proud palaces: young ladies who could be called truly beautiful. I have told you how Orlando found a damsel in the cave and how he asked her who had imprisoned her there. Now I come to what, after more than one sob had prevented her, she told the count about her troubles, in a sweet and very soft voice, as briefly as she could.

"Although," she said, "I am sure to be punished for speaking to you, sir—because as soon as she can, that old woman will tell the man who keeps me here—I do not want to hide the truth from you even though my life hangs in the balance. He might very well kill me for speaking. I cannot expect anything better from him. He might as well do it. I hope he does.

"My name is Isabella, and I was the daughter of the unfortunate Maricoldo, King of Galicia. I say I *was*, because I am not his any more, but only a child of pain, suffering and sorrow. It was all Love's fault; Love is so treacherous, so sweet in the beginning, you know, while he's secretly plotting to trick and deceive us. Once I lived happily—noble, young, rich, honorable and fair. Now I am vile, poor and unhappy. My lot simply could not be worse. But I want you to know about the cause, the root from which all this evil sprouted up around me to torment me. Even if you do not help me, your sympathy will mean something to me.

"Twelve months ago now, my father held a tournament in Bayonne. News of it brought knights from many lands to compete. Among them was the son of the great King of Scotland. Whether Love pointed him out to me, or his own virtues spoke for him after I saw him perform wonders of knighthood in the field, I fell in love with him. Before I knew it, I was no longer my own. And yet, though Love simply forced me to love him, I was always sure that I had not set my heart on an unworthy man, but on the worthiest and handsomest man alive in the world today; Zerbino was braver and more beautiful than all the other lords.

"And he said he loved me, and I believe he did. He was as ardent as I. We had someone to use as a go-between, so that even when we could not see each other, we were together in spirit. But when the tournament was over, my Zerbino had to go back to Scotland. If you know what loving is like, you know very well how sad I was when he left. I thought about him day and night, and of course the separation bothered him no less. He did not try to forget me; he tried to find a way to have me with him again. Of course he could not ask my father for my hand. The difference of our faiths prevented that, he being Christian and I Saracen.

"So he had to carry me off in secret.

"Now, outside our rich capital, which rises among green hills beside the Atlantic, I had a lovely garden with a view of the surrounding hills and all the sea. And this place seemed to provide the opportunity to achieve what our faiths prohibited. And he let me know the plan he had made for our happiness: near Santa Marta he had hidden a galley with armed men under

the command of Odorico of Biscay, a master of warfare on land and sea.

"Zerbino could not come to me himself, because
just then his old father sent him to help the King of
France, so he sent this Odorico in his place—his very
best friend, he was sure—and he certainly ought to
have been a friend, if you can earn friends with gifts
and favors. He was to come on an armed ship, at the
time we agreed on, to take me away. And at last the
time came, the day I longed for, when I was to let
him find me in my garden.

"In the dark, accompanied by men who were brave
at sea or in battle, Odorico came silently up a stream
near the town, and silently to my garden. And they
took me down to the galley before the town had any
news of it! Some of my unarmed servants fled, some
were killed, and a few were taken captive with me. So I
abandoned my country with more joy than I can tell,
hoping soon to have Zerbino.

"We had no sooner passed Mongia, however, when
we were assailed by a wind from the shore to the east,
disturbing the calm air and the water, raising waves up
to the sky. And then a northwest wind leaped up and
grew hourly fiercer and fiercer, with so much force
that it was impossible to tack with it and lowering
the sails was no help. The sailors even took down the
mast and lashed it on the deck between the benches.
They even jettisoned the superstructures at the stern
and the prow. But whatever they did, we were driven
in spite of it all toward the sharp rocks near La
Rochelle. Our only hope of not being driven by the
cruel tempest on that shore lay in God, because that
wind drove us faster than an arrow shot from a bow.

"Odorico, that Biscayan, saw the danger and took
our only, our last, dangerous chance: we abandoned
ship in a skiff. He had it lowered with me in it, too.

He made me go with him. Two other men joined us, as he ordered; most or all of the others would have joined us, too, if Odorico and his friends had let them. But they held them back with their swords, and cut the ropes, and we were free.

"We were thrown to safety on the shore, only us four who were in the skiff. All the others perished with the ship, which split on the rocks out at sea. And the sea got all our goods, too. Well, I got to shore and I stretched out my hands and gave thinks to eternal Providence, to infinite Love, that the fury of the Atlantic had not prevented me from seeing Zerbino ever again. Even though I had lost clothes and jewels and other dear things on the ship, I did not mind the ocean's getting everything, because I still had the hope of having my Zerbino.

"There were no signs of any people where we landed. There was no inn and there was not even any path. Only the hills, with the forests above always tossing in the mistral and the sea always beating there below.

"And here Love, the cruel tyrant, who always breaks his promises and always tries to ruin all our plans, tragically and dishonorably changed all my relief to pain, all my good to bad: because that friend Zerbino believed in burned with desire, while his friendship and loyalty froze.

"Whether he already hungered for me at sea and did not dare show it, or his appetite was first roused in the convenience of that lonely shore, he fully intended to satisfy it right then and there. But first, he had to dispose of one of the two men who were with us in the boat. That one was a Scot named Almonio. He was always very faithful to Zerbino, and Zerbino had recommended him to Odorico as a perfect knight. So he had to get rid of him. Odorico said it would be disgraceful to bring me into La Rochelle on foot, and asked Almonio to go ahead of us, get a horse and meet us on the way to town.

"Almonio saw no harm in this and set out right away for the town, not more than six miles away, through the woods, we were sure, though we could see nothing but those woods, beside that wild sea.

"Odorico let the other man know what he was going to do, because he could not think of a way to get rid of him as well, or had great confidence in him, or for both reasons. That one, the one who remained with us, was Corebo of Bilbao. He had been brought up with Odorico. So that traitor convinced himself that he could confide in him, expecting him to love his friend's pleasure more than justice. But Corebo wouldn't listen to him. He was quite disgusted. He called him a traitor and argued with him, and finally opposed him with deeds as well as words.

"Both of them burned with anger and showed it by drawing their swords; they drew their swords and I fled up the hillside to the deep, dark woods.

"It wasn't long before Odorico was after me. He was very good at dueling and in a few strokes he left Corebo on the ground for dead and started after me. Love gave him wings, I believe, so that I would not get away. And then Love showed him how to flatter me and plead with me to get me to comply with his desire.

"But all in vain. I was firm. I would die rather than give in. And after he had tried all his prayers, and threats, and they did not help him, he resorted to simple force. As for me, I kept reminding him how Zerbino trusted him, and trusted me in his hands, but that did me no good. When I knew I'd thrown away my prayers in vain, he being so persistent, vile and greedy, and coming at me like a hungry bear, I defended myself with my hands and feet, and even used my nails and teeth against him. I scratched his face and I bit him, and I also screamed as loudly as I could.

"I don't know whether they heard my screams. My screams must have carried for a mile or more, in spite of the surf and the wind in the trees. Or it might have been just because they always run down to the shore when a ship breaks up on the rocks.

"At any rate, I saw a crowd appear on the hilltop, and they were hurrying toward us. And when the Biscayan saw them coming, he gave up and turned and ran. So they were a great help against that ingrate, of course, but as they say, it was a fall out of the frying pan into the fire. It is true that they have not been so wicked as to attempt to violate me. But that is not because there is any good in them, but only because they know that if they keep me as I am, a virgin, they can sell me at a better price.

"It is over eight months that I have been buried here. I have lost all hope of my Zerbino. Because I gather from what they say that they have already promised me and sold me to a slaver who is going to take me to the Sultan in the Levant."

So spoke the gentle girl, her angelic voice often broken by sobs and sighs. Even poisonous snakes would have been moved to pity. And as she finished telling her troubles, maybe easing her pain, about twenty men came into the cavern, some armed with hunting spears and some with billhooks.

The first man looked pitiless, and he was. He had only one eye, and it was dark and grim. His other eye had been put out by a blow that had scarred his nose and his jaw as well. Seeing the knight inside the den with the fair virgin, he turned to his comrades and said, "Lo! A new bird in the net, and I didn't even set it for him!"

Then he said to the count, "I never saw a man more accommodating than you at so opportune a moment. I don't know if you realized it, I don't know if you thought of it yourself or if somebody told you, but I can very well use such fair arms, and this pretty dark cloak of yours, too. You have come just in time to fill my needs."

Orlando gave the robber a bitter smile and answer, saying, "I will sell them to you at a price that merchants do not list."

Orlando was standing beside the fire, and out of it he snatched a big, smoking, blazing log, then threw it, and it happened to hit the highwayman right across the eyes. It did more damage on the left side, blinding the one good eye. But it did not merely blind him; it added his name to those of the evil spirits Chiron keeps in the burning lake in the Inferno.

There was a big table in the cave. It stood on one thick, unpolished stump. It was two spans thick, and square, and wide enough for the thief and all his followers to sit there at one time. As nimbly as you see the Spaniards throw their reed darts for sport, Orlando hurled that heavy table at the mob. It broke chests, bellies, heads, legs and arms; some men died and some were left crippled. If you drop a big rock on a knot of grass snakes sunning themselves and polishing their scales when winter is over, who could account for all their injuries, and give the details? You can only say it squashes some, and some are dead, and some cannot move forward but only writhe, and a few, to whom the stars were kinder, go coiling away. The table did terrible damage. No wonder; it was Orlando who threw it.

Those whom the table hurt little or not at all, and Turpin writes that there were exactly seven of them, tried to run. But Orlando was at the exit before them.

He took them without a fight. He tied their hands tightly with rope he found right there in the forest den. Then he dragged them outside. Near the cave grew an old sorb-apple tree. Orlando lopped the branches short with his sword and hanged the men there for the ravens. He did not need a gibbet to purge the world of those pests; the tree provided the hooks where Orlando hanged them.

The old woman, the highwaymen's friend, ran weeping with her hands in her hair through the labyrinthine woods and thickets. After long, intricate, hard traveling, with heavy steps but still driven on by fear, she met a knight on the bank of a river. But I put off telling who he was and return to the other woman . . .

. . . the young woman, who begged the paladin not to leave her there alone, and said she would follow him anywhere, wherever he was going. Courteously, Orlando comforted her, and after pale Aurora appeared, adorned with her garland of roses and her purple robe, making it light enough to see that all the thieves were dead, he left the place and took Isabella with him. They rode together for many days without finding anything worth noting here, until at last they saw a knight being led prisoner along the road. Who he was, I will say later; I have to leave Orlando and Isabella for another character you would just as soon hear about anyway . . .

. . . Bradamante, daughter of Aimone, whom I left not long ago, weak with love and grief.

That fair lady, longing in vain for Ruggiero to come back to her, was waiting for him in Marseilles. Almost daily she harassed the pagans who went robbing on hill and plain throughout Languedoc and Provence round about, fairly doing her duty as a good ruler and as a perfect knight. But otherwise, she merely waited, living in constant fear for him.

On one of those days when she stayed apart, mourning alone, there came to her the enchantress who had taken him the ring, the medicine that cured his heart of Alcina's wound.

When Bradamante saw her coming without him, after such a long time, she turned pale and shook so much that she could hardly keep her feet. But the gentle witch came before her smiling when she saw how afraid she was, comforting her with the happy face of one who brings good news.

"Do not be afraid about Ruggiero, lady," she said. "He is alive and well and loves you as before. But he is not yet free. Your enemy has stolen his freedom again, and you have to climb into the saddle and follow me right now if you want him. If you follow, I will show you where Ruggiero is imprisoned this time to be freed by you once more."

She went on to tell her about the magic errors Atlante had fabricated for him: how he simulated Bradamante's own fair face, pretended she was captured by a wicked giant, and led Ruggiero into the enchanted house where the illusion vanished before him; and how he detained with similar impostures and deceits all the knights and ladies who came there.

"As soon as you arrive in the area near the enchanted palace," Melissa told Bradamante, "the enchanter will come to meet you—with all Ruggiero's features. And his evil power will make it seem that someone, or something, of greater strength than Ruggiero is conquering him, so that you will go to help him where, with the others, he will keep you. In order not to fall into the trap where so many and so many are fallen, be advised: however much *like* Ruggiero he appears to you, begging for your help, do not believe him, but kill him as quickly as you can. Do not be afraid you will be killing Ruggiero; you will be killing your enemy and his, the one who is keeping you apart.

"Now, I know very well that it will seem hard to kill someone who looks just like your Ruggiero. But do not trust your eyes. The magic will deceive them and hide the truth. You must be determined, before I lead you to that wood, not to change your mind when you see him. For you will remain without Ruggiero forever, if through vile weakness you let the magician live."

The brave lady knight, with the intention of killing the deceiver as advised, was quick to take arms and follow Melissa; she knew very well how trustworthy and faithful Melissa was. And Melissa led her, now through tilled fields, now through forest land, on a great journey in great haste, always trying to alleviate the wearisome road with agreeable talk.

Most of the time, Melissa told her about those excellent princes and glorious demigods who were to descend from her and Ruggiero. Since the enchantress knew all the secrets of the eternal gods, she could foretell everything for many ages.

"O prudent guide," Bradamante said to her, "you have already told me about so many of the men of my posterity. Perhaps you could say something about some of the women, if you consider any of them fair and virtuous."

And the courteous enchantress answered her at length.

While Melissa told Bradamante about the greater part of her future race, to her great comfort, time and again the witch repeated her warning about the art that had drawn Ruggiero into the magic palace. And when she was near that abode of the evil old man, she halted and would not go nearer to risk being seen by him—and to see we know not what.

Once again, near the sphere of Atlante's magic influence, she advised the girl as she had done a thousand times before. Then she left her alone.

And Bradamante had not traveled more than two miles down a narrow path before she saw the thing that resembled her Ruggiero. He was on horseback, and on either side he had a cruel-looking giant attacking him, each one pressing him so hard that he was near his death. When the girl saw him, looking just like Ruggiero in every way and in such great danger, her faith in Melissa quickly turned to suspicion and she forsook all her good intentions. She suddenly was afraid that Melissa might hate Ruggiero for some reason of which she knew nothing, and sought with this clever plot to have him done to death by her who loved him so. Where was the anti-magical ring? Suppose Ruggiero did indeed have it, and Melissa herself could not harm him, but wanted him killed?

Bradamante said to herself, "Isn't he Ruggiero? Isn't it he, always in my heart, whom I now see with my eyes at last? And if I do not see him and know him now, who can I ever see and know? How can I trust someone else's word instead of my own eyes? For even if I could not see him so well, even if I could not see him at all, my heart tells me he is near."

While she was thinking this, she heard the voice that seemed to be Ruggiero's calling her, begging for her help; and at the same time she saw him spur his horse and loose the reins, while both of his ferocious enemies ran after him. They were on foot, but their legs were so long that she was sure they would overtake him soon; even though they did not seem to be running at full speed, they seemed to keep close behind him and his horse would not gallop that fast for very long. The lady did not hesitate. She was already riding after them, until they led her to the magic palace.

She no sooner entered the gate than she was hopelessly submerged, overwhelmed in the common error. She ransacked the palace, upstairs and down, indoors and out, all in vain. She did not stop looking day or night, so strong was the spell. And the enchanter had cast the spell so cleverly that she often saw Ruggiero, and even spoke with him, but they could not recognize each other. Now Atlante's trap was full, the plot complete.

And there we must leave her. Don't worry, though. She will not be there forever. When it is time for Bradamante to be freed, I will have her freed—and Ruggiero, too.

Since a change of diet improves the appetite, it seems to me that my story may be the less tedious the more it is varied. Or look at it this way: I have to weave many threads into the large tapestry I'm working on. So let me tell you how, outside the gates of Paris, King Agramante had the Moorish hosts assemble, in arms, before him, in order to see how many men he could call upon to destroy the gold lilies of France. He had lost a great many footmen and knights, not to mention their leaders; he had lost some of the best— from Spain, Libya and Ethiopia as well—and untold squadrons, even whole nations, were left wandering, without commanders. Now all the pagan forces were gathered for review, to be put in order. And to make up their losses, the kings of Spain and Africa had sent word back to their own lands, over the mountains and across the sea, and had summoned more and more infantry, cavalry and commanders.

I will put off to the next volume—with your permission, lord—the muster of the hosts.